A FORSYTH DUO

GAVIN MACDONALD

ISBN   978 – 1 – 326 – 24950 - 2

To Candy

who makes sure there are no errors in these books

Detective Chief Inspector Ian Forsyth Books

Death is my Mistress
The Crime Committee
My Frail Blood
Publish and be Dead
Swallow Them Up
Dishing The Dirt
A Family Affair
Playing Away
Bloody and Invisible Hand
The Truth in Masquerade
I Spy, I Die
A Bow at a Venture
Passport to Perdition
The Plaintive Numbers
The Root of all Evil
Pay Any Price
Murder at he Museum
Murder of an Unknown
The Long Arm
The Forsyth Saga
The Second Forsyth Saga
A Further Forsyth Saga
Double Jeopardy
Rendezvous with Death

Science Fiction:
Mysteries of Space and Time

Science Mystery
Amorphous

CONTENTS

FOREWORD

For this, the twenty fifth novel chronicling the exploits of Detective Chief Inspector Ian Forsyth, you get two cases for the price of one. The first occured fairly early in my association with him in the summer of 1979 and the second nearer the end of it in July of 1983. It may well be that I have chosen ithe first because I come out of it fairly well, not quite arriving at the correct solution but getting very close to it. The second is a good illustration of how Forsyth is successful because he notices things that escape the rest of us.

Forsyth is still somewhat of a legend in the Lothian and Boders Police Headquarters. Raw recruits are regaled with tales of his triumphs by grizzled veterans who, unfortunately, have added all sorts of improbable details to the original stories. The result of this is that the listeners come to believe that Forsyth never existed, that what they are hearing is an amalgum of all the outstanding successes of officers in the past.

I can assure them that Forsyth certainly existed. I .worked for the man for more years than I care to remember. And there is no need to add extraneous material to the cases that he solved. The deductions by which he solved his cases are brilliant enough without the need for any enhancement.

Not that he was an easy man to work with. He had his flaws, possibly more than most men. We often felt put upon when he piled routine work, which he hated, and was not much good at, on us. But we shared in the triumph when he solved a case and we knew that he fought for us ruthlessly when we got into trouble. And no-one ever asked to be moved from his squad.

It gave me great pleasure to relive these stirring times. I can only hope you get as much pleasure from reading about them.

Alistair MacRae,

Edinburgh, 2015.

THE CASE OF THE VANISHING VETERANS

CHAPTER 1

It was in the middle of the morning on a fine day in late August that we were called out to investigate the death of Norman Mathers. He had lived by himself in what had once been his parents' house in the old part of Liberton, not all that far from where my humble dwelling is situated, though the latter is in the newer area of that part of Edinburgh.

I drove Forsyth up from Fettes to Liberton which lies to the south of the city and is at a much higher elevation than the Police Headquarters. I was forced to park in the next street since there were so many vehicles cluttering up the rather narrow road. When we got to the house, we passed through the small garden at the front and entered the two-storey detached building to find DC Andy Beaumont awaiting us.

"Morning, sir," he said to the Chief. "The dead man's name is Norman Mathers. He was an accountant who worked for one of the morning papers, The *Edinburgh Daily Gleaner.* He looks to have been very badly tortured before they got round to killing him. You'll find Dr Hay with the body now."

"Then we had better join the good doctor," said Forsyth.

I have seen a fair number of bodies, in all sorts of condition, in my time. But the body in the sitting room was a bit of a shock. It was stark naked and was strapped to a chair and with a gag in its mouth. There were cigarette burns and bloody cuts on various parts of the body. A couple of the fingers on each hand appeared to have been broken. There was severe bruising on the face and body and the nose was clearly out of joint. The man who had probably been quite good looking and in good shape was now in a total mess. Dr Hay, the police surgeon, was examining the body and one of the forensic team was doing various tasks around the room. Both looked up as we entered.

Hay, the police surgeon, was in his late forties, a rotund figure who peered benevolently at the world through thick pebble spectacles. He was wearing the usual shapeless clothes and had, on his head, the battered old soft hat without which he was never seen. Rumour has it that he sleeps in these garments as well. He was reputed to have no interest in life other than medicine and the only thing that was alleged to stir his heart was the thrill of expectation at the moment when he had a knife poised to slice into the latest victim on his mortuary table. But he was one of the best quacks in the business and you could rely one hundred per cent on what he told you about a victim.

Hay came over to greet us, at the same time drawing from his pocket a cigar case from which he extracted one of the cheroots to which he was addicted. Having lit this, he inhaled with evident satisfaction a large lungful of the evil-smelling smoke and then beamed a warm smile contentedly at us.

"The more I examine dead bodies," he said, "the more I despair of my fellow human beings. We're supposed to be civilised. But the person who did this is a real bastard, more depraved than the worst animal."

"Did he die as a result of the torture he suffered," I asked, "or was he killed when he finally gave up the information that they were seeking?"

"It's anybody's guess as to what they got from him," Hay suggested. "But, if I had to make a wager on it, I would doubt that he gave them what they wanted. It looks as if his heart gave out before they had induced him to spill the beans."

"What time did all this happen?" I enquired.

"The torture must have lasted for quite a time. He died around 2am this morning, give or take an hour either way."

"Who found him?" I asked Beaumont.

"He was a bachelor. The woman who cleaned for

him, a Mrs Jennings, came in as usual this morning and found the body. After she had recovered from her hysterics, she called us. She's in the kitchen mopping up tea and biscuits to restore herself. Tea, I may say, that has been fortified with just a wee drop of Mr Mathers' finest whisky."

"Is there anything here," Forsyth enquired of the forensic expert, "that you have found and that we should know about?"

"Not a thing," he replied. "The killer wore gloves and probably some sort of coverall suit. He's left nothing that I can find."

"Then we will go and have a talk with the cleaning lady."

Mrs Jennings was a small, stout lady of indeterminate age, dressed in a sweater and trousers and with a lined face and black hair. She was seated in a comfortable chair, with a teacup in her hand, and had obviously been regaling the uniformed plod who was keeping an eye on her with scurrilous stories of the goings-on of the families for whom she did. She eyed us with a certain amount of suspicion as we entered. We had obviously not impressed her as important purveyors of law.

"I gather that you looked after this house for Mr Mathers," Forsyth said to her.

"That I did these five years past and never a word of complaint from him," the lady replied. "And then to find him in that terrible state. I dinna think that I'll ever get the sight of him tied to that chair out of my mind."

"It must have been a great shock for you to find him in that state."

"That it was. I almost fainted at that first sight of him. I had to sit down in a chair for a few minutes to get my senses back."

"Did Mr Mathers ever entertain men with whom he had violent arguments?"

"He wisna that kind of man at all. Very gentle he was. And his few friends were the same. I never met one that would do yon to him. Mind you, I don't think he fancied the ladies if you get my meaning. And that kind sometimes mixes with awful funny people."

"Did he have anything valuable, such as a lot of money or jewellry, hidden somewhere in the house?" I enquired.

"Never. He kept his money in the bank like the rest of us. And he wisna into jewels. And he didn't have anything else that was all that valuable in the house, hidden or otherwise."

"So why were they torturing him?"

"There are some funny folk around that like inflicting

pain."

"I would like you to look around the house with D C Beaumont," said Forsyth, "to see if anything is missing. And it would be helpful if you could give him a list of Mr Mathers' friends with their addresses, if you know them, or where they worked."

"I think you'll find all that in his address book. I'll show Mr Beaumont where it is and try to tell him who all the people are."

"That would be most helpful."

When Andy had left with the lady in tow, I turned to the Chief.

"I would doubt that his sexual preferences led to this," I said. "It looks as if someone wanted something from him very badly. Maybe one of his friends can tell us what that was likely to be."

"You are probably correct. Get Beaumont to share out with the other two the list of friends from the address book. We will go and see what his colleagues at the office of *The Daily Gleaner* have to say."

The newspaper operated from premises a little way off Nicolson Street, so we drove back there from Liberton. The editor was a small bustling man called Edward Harding who saw us as soon as we arrived. He took the news of Mathers' death hard.

"I can't believe it," he said. "Norman was a good accountant. But he was the last man in the world that I would have guessed would die a violent death. Some of the people who worked with him called him Normal Mathers because his views on everything were so utterly predictable."

"And you can't think of anything," I asked, "that someone would want from him so badly that they would torture him to death?"

"Not a thing. The mind boggles at the thought of Norman having anything that people would want that badly."

"And he hasn't, in the course of his work here, come across anyone on these premises who was fiddling expenses or doing anything else that might be considered illegal?"

"He hasn't unearthed anything going on in this office or elsewhere."

"Perhaps we should have a word with his secretary," suggested Forsyth. "A secretary often knows more about her boss than anyone else."

Gladys Lawson was a middle-aged lady, well dressed and attractive but somewhat demure. She received the news of Mathers' death in startled silence and needed a little time to recover. When she had drunk some water from a glass that I fetched and wiped tears from her eyes, she answered our questions.

"I can't believe that he died in that way," she admitted. "He was the last man one would expect to be mixed up in the sort of business that would lead to a violent death. He was the nicest man I ever met."

"So you don't know of anything valuable he might possess that someone would wish to get his hands on?" I asked.

"He wasn't all that well off. And he didn't go around second-hand shops where he might have picked up a long lost treasure. He was unlikely to have anything in that house of great value."

"And he hadn't got up anyone's nose in a big way recently?"

"He wasn't that kind of man at all. He didn't produce that sort of emotion in other people."

No-one else in the newspaper office had any useful information. It was all pretty baffling.

We were directed to his best friend, John Summers, who was a tall, thin man with a diffident manner who worked in the Council Offices. But his information matched that that we had already received.

"He was a very private man," he told us. "He had few intimate friends, He found it difficult to relate to other people. We hit it off because we had a mutual interest in the theatre. He certainly had no possessions that were worth a lot of money or that would be attractive to a criminal. And he didn't have any valuable knowledge that someone would wish to torture him to get at. I can only imagine that it was some sad, demented person who had formed some wild notion that Norman was the devil incarnate and had to be exorcised."

That night Forsyth's team, but without him of course, had a session in the bar that we frequent after work. It lies half-way between the Police Headquarters at Fettes and the Crematorium. And we were occupying our usual table which has no other within earshot so that there is no danger that any of our words of wisdom will reach flapping ears and appear in garbled form in the next day's *Scotsman* or *Daily Gleaner.* I bought pints of heavy for three of us and a gin and tonic for the fourth and, once we had all slaked our thirst, I gave an account of all that Forsyth and I had learned that day and then invited the others to report on their findings.

Each member of the team informed me that he had visited the friends of Mathers that he had been allocated, but had been told the same story by all of them. None of them, apart from Summers, had been all that close to Mathers and would not necessarily have known his more intimate secrets. But all said that he had been the nicest and kindest of men. There was nothing in his life that would suggest that he would die a violent death after being tortured. And no-one had any idea that he would possess the sort of knowledge that someone would be prepared to torture him to death in order to try to get information about it.

We decided that his death was a mystery and was likely to remain so. With no clues, there was nothing to work on so, unless further information turned up, which at that time seemed unlikely, the death of Mathers was fated to stay a mystery forever.

CHAPTER 2

It was ten days later that I got rung up from the front desk by Sergeant Anderson. He informed me that another dead body that had been tortured had been found and that it was waiting to be investigated by the police. And, since the Forsyth team had been asked to deal with the previous torture victim, it was fitting that we should handle the second one as well. It made sense. So I sent the rest of the team on ahead to get things organised and went to let the Chief know that his deductive abilities were once more required.

The victim had been found in the tenement flat that he occupied at the lower end of Leith Walk. I parked in a side street and we walked round to where a crowd had gathered outside the building. A uniformed plod, once he recognised the great man, hastened to make a way through the crowd to let us get to the tenement and we mounted the stairs to the first floor where DC Andy Beaumont was waiting in the entrance to one of the four flats that came off the landing.

"Morning, sir," he said to Forsyth. "The victim is a Tom Murphy. He did labouring jobs in a factory near the harbour. He has been treated exactly like the last dead one that we saw a few days ago. He has been bound and gagged and then subjected to torture. He lived on his own since his wife left him a year or so back. As far as we have discovered, no-one heard anything during the night. Or, if they did, they did nothing about it and are not admitting to any knowledge of the events that took place here now."

"How did the killer manage to get into the flat?" I enquired.

"The front door is only on a Yale lock. He probably used a strip of plastic to turn back the lock and get in."

"Who found the body?" I asked.

"The woman who lives in the flat next door gets paid a small amount by Murphy to keep his flat clean. She has a key to the place so that she can get in as necessary. When she went in this morning, she found him tied to a chair and very dead."

"Where is she now?"

"I let her go back to her flat under the eyes of a uniform."

"We will see her later," said Forsyth. "First, we had better have a look at the body."

Andy directed us to the kitchen which was quite small and, besides a cooker, contained a microwave and a fridge,a table, a quartet of chairs and little else. Tied to one of the chairs was the body of an elderly man with a gag in his mouth. He had been cut in several places, had burns on various parts of his body and a couple of his fingers had been broken. Dr Hay was just straightening up from an examination of the body as we entered. He came over at once to greet us, lighting up one of his cheroots as he did so.

"It looks to be the same sadistic bastard who did this as did the last one," he said, puffing out a cloud of unpleasant smoke. "I doubt that this one lasted as long as the other did before he gave up his life. He hadn't kept himself in as good nick as the last one and wouldn't have coped with the pain so well."

"When did all this sadistic torturing take place?" I asked.

"I reckon that he died around midnight. The torturing didn't last all that long before he gave up the ghost. And, since there is nothing else useful that I can tell you, I will get on my way. I have a lot of calls still to make this morning."

And, with that, he picked up his bag and was on his way, leaving behind the echo of a tuneless whistle and some highly unpleasant smoke.

The man from forensics had nothing of interest for us and, after a look around the kitchen and the rest of the flat, which yielded no clues whatsoever, we went next door to interview Mrs Cuthbertson, the lady who had found the body. She turned out to be a tall woman with a narrow face, as thin as a rake, clad in a faded skirt and an old knitted jumper.

"It gave me a hell of a shock to find him like that," she told us. "He was a mean bastard but he didna deserve to end like yon."

"Who was likely to want to do that sort of thing to him?" I asked.

"I dinna ken anyone who would treat him like yon. He didna mix wi' folks who would think of doing that sort of thing to a body."

"I gather that his wife left him some time ago," I said. "Would any of her friends or relatives feel badly enough about how he treated her to want to take a bit of a revenge on him?"

"His wife was a nice lady," she insisted, "who wouldna dream of getting someone to do yon to him. She left him because he got drunk too often, could be more than a wee bit aggressive when he had too much liquor in him and was spending too much of her money on the booze. I dinna think that she bore him any great grudge. She was just glad to be on her own again without him as a millstone around her neck."

"Had Mr Murphy an acquaintance called Norman Mathers?" asked Forsyth.

Mrs Cuthbertson gave the matter some thought.

"I dinna ken the man," she said at length. "And I canna

remember him ever mentioning the name."

"Mr Mathers worked for a newspaper," I informed the lady.

"He's no likely to have kent him then," she said firmly. "He had difficulty in reading anything. So he wisna into the papers."

"Perhaps the two of them met at some activity they had in common?" I suggested.

"The only activities that Tom indulged in were boozing down at the local pub and watching the Hibs getting beat at Easter Road," she insisted.

"And Mathers didn't do either of these things," I said thoughtfully.

We talked to others who lived in the tenement and to the people who had been named as the friends with whom Murphy drank and with whom he went to the football matches. But the story from all of them was the same. Murphy had had no interest in anything but booze and football. No-one had ever heard him speak of Norman Mathers. And no-one could imagine that Murphy would have known of anything of such great value that someone would torture him to get at it. It was admitted that he occasionally did the odd job for one of the local villains. But everyone was adamant that Murphy had had enough sense not to do anything as stupid as hanging on to money or goods that were the property of the villain. It was all very dispiriting. There seemed no reason at all why Murphy would have been tortured and there seemed no connection at all between Murphy and the earlier victim, Norman Mathers.

On the way back to Fettes, I quizzed Forsyth as to what he made of it all. He took a little time to answer, no doubt because he never liked to admit that he was baffled by a case. But eventually he admitted that he was as completely at sea as I was. Not that that gave me any satisfaction. If the Chief was baffled, what chance was there for the rest of us mere mortals to see light in the darkness. None the less, the team had a session to discuss the case at the end of the day.

It may cause surprise that we were discussing the case in a pub and not in Headquarters with Forsyth in attendance, but it is common practice with us. On our previous session in the pub, we had traded reports on what had seemed an isolated incident. But, with the second killing turning this into a major case, the sitauation had altered. Any team of Forsyth's that I run will always meet in the pub of an evening during the course of a major investigation in order to discuss the case. And there is a good reason why we do it in the pub and not in the nick in the company of the great man.

Forsyth always plays his cards close to his chest. He suffered some little time ago an acrimonious divorce from his former wife where lots of things that he had said came back in a form that told against him and, probably because of that unedifying experience, he does not ever wish it to be known that he has said or done anything that might be considered to be wrong. And, having gone down that route, he has now got himself into a position where he wants to be regarded as infallible at all times. So he keeps his thoughts to himself until he is absolutely sure that he has got everything right. In consequence, we mere mortals work in the dark unless he condescends to come down from Mount Olympus and give us some instructions. These may, or may not, make sense, but we follow them to the letter. And later we discover why we were required to do these things and they all slot into place. But we never know what his thinking is until he has solved the case and is prepared to dazzle us all with the brilliance of his reasoning.

Most of those who work for Forsyth accept this philosophically, since his method of working has brought spectacular results. But, a few years previously a rather bolshy Detective Constable on the team complained to him that he was unhappy at being treated like a cypher and kept totally in the dark. Forsyth's reply was simple. He pointed out that his method worked very successfully. So, only if one of his team arrived at the solution of a mystery before, or indeed even at the same time as, he did would he think of changing his *modus operandi.* He also added that, should such an unlikely event ever occur, he would proclaim the triumph of his minion from the rooftops and would also present the successful solver with a crate of the finest malt whisky.

Since that time, all teams have attempted to arrive at the solution of a major case before Forsyth is able to do so. This is not because we wish him to change his method of working which has been spectacularly successful, though a little more enlightenment during the course of an investigation would be very welcome. But we are intent on winning that crate of malt whisky in order to show him that, at least on one occasion, we can be as brilliant as he is and can beat him to the punch. I have to confess humbly that so far we have not been able to achieve our strived-for ambition.

So that evening found us in the pub. I had bought what would be the first round and had offered cigarettes to the others. Two had accepted and lit up while the third, who didn't indulge, had moved his chair slightly away from the blossoming clouds of smoke.

Once we had all slaked our thirst, I got us down to

business. I started by telling them everything that Forsyth and I had come across that day. I believe in letting every member of a squad know all that has been discovered. The rawest recruit is as capable of coming up with the bright idea that solves a case as is a grizzled veteran. But he cannot do that unless he is aware of all that has been discovered.

After I had finished my spiel, I asked Andy Beaumont to let us know what he had discovered. Andy is a little on the short side for a policeman but he has two qualities that make him invaluable to the Force. The first is that he can pass for an average Joe anywhere. Once he's left you, you find it difficult to think of any characteristic with which to describe him. He can melt into a crowd and find out what's going on without anyone giving him a second glance. His build is average and he has an ordinary, unmemorable, innocent face, mousy brown hair and clothes indistinguishable from his neighbour's.

His second great virtue is that he could worm information from a tailor's dummy. When you talk to him, you get the impression that he's drinking in every word and that what you are saying is the most important thing in the world. He's the perfect listener and that, allied to his ready sympathy and ordinary appearance, means that neighbours, tradesmen and servants open their heart to him when any other copper would find them silent and resentful. He had been talking to people in the pub that Murphy frequented.

"I couldn't find anyone," he told us, "who wasn't gobsmacked by the way that Murphy died. He was just an ordinary bloke and no-one believed that he possessed any knowledge that someone would torture him to get out of him. And no-one had ever heard any mention of Mathers from him."

He picked up his pint and had a swallow.

"I suggested," he went on, "that he might have got up the noses of some fans of the other teams, particularly the great Ednburgh rivals of Hibs, the Hearts. But that was poopooed. His pals said that he was much more likely to have a drink with a Hearts fan than come to blows with him."

"So we are still as devoid of any notion as to what these killings are all about as ever," I said. "What about you, Sid? Did you get anything?"

Sid Fletcher is a tall, lean, cadaverous individual, forty years old and with a gloomy expression and thinning, black hair. He's been the longest of all of us on Forsyth's team and will remain there till retirement. His many years in the force have convinced him that it will always be his fate to be the one left holding the short straw, and his wife leaving him, unable to stand the amount of time she was left on her own and the cold shouldering by some of the neighbours, did nothing to lessen that view. But he carries on his work with fierce determination to show that he will not let the fates get him down. And he is fiercely loyal to Forsyth who is the one rock to which he can cling in the shifting sands of life. But he is also the least bright of the individuals on the team.

"Murphy, as Andy has just said, was a member of the Hibs' supporters group," he said. "Him and a fellow called Desmond Bannon went to all the games together. I talked to him and, indeed, all the other Hibs fans who knew him. Like Andy, I got nowhere. No-one, including Bannon, could think of any reason why the killer would want to try to get something out of Murphy. He had never had a penny to his name in his whole life and hadn't been connected with any group that would have had the brains to get their hands on a large sum of cash, legally or otherwise They were all totally astonished that he had finished up in the way that he did."

He stopped, picked up his glass and had a sup of his pint.

I looked across at Martin Jenkins. Jenkins was, at that time, the most recent addition to our little band of crime busters, the very epitome of clean-limbed youth. He is tall and spare, snappily dressed, with a keen, eager face and wavy hair trimmed to regulation length. He is the one who would not defile his body by allowing tobacco smoke to percolate through it. He would make a good model for a more youthful, more innocent Sherlock Holmes from the time before he met the good Dr Watson. A recent recruit, armed with a degree and convinced that a Chief Constable's baton was already nestling in his knapsack and would be brought into use in record time, he gives all the appearance of a trained bloodhound tugging impatiently at the leash. Most of his superiors tend to treat his enthusiasm indulgently, while missing no opportunity to rub his nose in the messier parts of the routine of police work. But he brings out the worst in Forsyth who no doubt recognises in the young man certain of his own less endearing qualities.

"I went through all the inhabitants of the tenement," he explained, "getting their views on Murphy. I reckon that most of them are involved in criminal activities of one sort or another. So they are not the keenest of people to help the police with their enquiries. But it was clear that they all had the same view of Murphy. He was a feckless man who tried to enjoy his simple life without any thought to what others, such as his former wife, might want. He had no interests except drinking and football and seemed to have no ambition whatsoever."

He finished and picked up his glass of gin and tonic and had a swallow. No pint of heavy for Jenkins. It just didn't fit his image.

It was obvious that Jenkins couldn't get his head round how anyone could live the way that Murphy had. He was an ambitious man himself and couldn't understand how others could live without goals to aim for. He really had little understanding of how most of his fellows lived their lives.

"And no-one had ever heard of any mention of Mathers from Murphy," he concluded.

"Has Forsyth got any ideas?" asked Fletcher.

"Not a one," I admitted. "Or at least, he wasn't telling any ideas that he had to me. And he certainly has no notion of why these people are being tortured or what the connection may be between such disparate people as Mathers and Murphy."

"So what are we supposed to do?" enquired Beaumont.

"The only thing that we can do," I replied, "is to rack our brains to see if we can come up with what ties Mathers and Murphy together. Apart from that, I don't think that there is anything that we can do."

Jenkins bought a round so that he could slope off when he wanted to. Drinking in a pub is no t his notion of the high life. He knows that he has to join us at these sessions but it is not how he would choose to spend his time.

We discussed other matters for a time but, when Fletcher offered another round, both Jenkins and I declined. The other two were happy to have a more prolonged drinking session and began by also ordering some food. The wives of both men had left them, a fate that occurs to quite a few policemen. So they preferred to spend the evening with a congenial companion rather than have a takeaway in front of the tele. But Jenkins and I had better things to do. We parted outside the pub and went our separate ways.

As I approached my house in Liberton, I realised that the lights were on in the kitchen. My immediate thought was not that burglars were inside intent on removing from me all my treasured possessions. My assumption was that a meal was being prepared for me by a lady called Anna Hyslop.

Anna is an ex-policewoman who got fed up with the sexist attitude she had to put up with from the large collection of male chauvinist pigs found in the force, left, did an accountancy degree at the University, finished with first class honours and a handful of prizes and now pulls in a hell of a lot more of the readies than she would be getting if she had stayed in the police and a good deal more than I was earning.

We hadn't got together when she was in the police. Our paths had hardly crossed. We ran into each other at a party while she was a student and she took to me, not only because of my good looks and ready wit, if you are prepared to believe I have these, but also when she found that I sympathised with what she'd had to put up with while still on the payroll. Macho maleness is not one of my things and I have always made sure that any woman with whom I worked was protected as far as possible from the worst of the excesses that male chauvinists tend to pile on them. Since I also found her attractive, intelligent and interested in other things than booze and sex, which seems to be what fills most students' minds these days, we'd got on like a house on fire. All right, we indulged in sex and it was an important part of our relationship, but it wasn't the be-all and end-all of our existence.

We had an easy-going relationship. She understood from past experience that there were times in a policeman's life when he had to work all the hours God gave him for days on end, and it didn't bother me that she whipped off to all sorts of locations to look to the needs of her customers and that she attended conferences in all sorts of exotic and very up-market places. We were both happy with a relationship that tied us only loosely together and had done nothing about making it more binding. We got together when we felt like it, which was normally quite often, and enjoyed each other's company just as much as the love-making. I had a key to her flat and she one to my house but neither of us imposed on the other. She misses the type of police work that had caused her to join the force in the first place and which she only had a chance to dip her toe into, and envies me my job as a Detective Sergeant, particularly as I work under a whiz kid like Forsyth. I was sure that she had heard of the latest torture victim and that I would be roundly interrogated and probed for details after I had been put into a good mood by the meal that she was preparing.

When I entered the house, she came out of the kitchen, kissed me, put into my hand a glass of chilled Sauvignon Blanc and told me to rest my weary bones in an armchair in the sitting room until she could join me. I was only too happy to do what I was told.

I gave her the few details that I had about the case at the end of the dinner, which had been first class, as we sat in the sitting room and finished the wine that I had served with the meal, since I knew that what I told her would go no further. She was intrigued and made some wild suggestions about what the connection between the two victims might have been, suggestions that I treated with the utmost respect. We discussed the possibilities for a while. But it was not long before desire overcame us and we retired to the bedroom and to sexual delights.

CHAPTER 3

Since I have given pen portraits of the other members of the team, perhaps I ought now to say a bit about the two most important members, namely Forsyth and me.

Ian Forsyth is imposing figure, an adjective that can also be applied to the way in which he deals with the hired help. He is 6' 4" with a large-boned, quite athletic frame which he keeps in reasonable nick with exercise and golf. A shock of blonde hair stands up above the broad forehead that crowns his long, rather distinguished face and a luxuriant moustache adorns, to be kind about it, his upper lip.

Forsyth's origins are somewhat obscure though I gather that he was born somewhere in the Highlands to a reasonably well-off family, but that he was educated at an exclusive public school in Edinburgh and then at the University there. What qualification he finished up with, I don't know, but I would expect it to have been a first class honours degree in something like the old-style Mathematics and Natural Philosophy Arts course. That would be consistent with both his logical mind and the fact that he is interested, and very well read, in the Arts. He was married at quite an early age but the union didn't turn out too well and ended in a very acrimonious divorce. This may explain his secretiveness and his unwillingness to leave himself open to criticism or to be shown to be in the wrong in any matter. He now lives alone, very well looked after by a housekeeper who is not only competent but an excellent cook. He enjoys a social life that includes golf at one of the more exclusive courses, bridge at one of the local clubs in Edinburgh, concerts and the theatre and allows him to mix with the great and the good in the higher echelons of Edinburgh society. We don't see all that much of him outside working hours though we are invited round to his house in a fairly exclusive area of Edinburgh for dinner from time to time and are always well looked after, superbly fed and supplied with a sufficiency of excellent wine and spirits.

It is not clear why Forsyth chose the police force as a career. He would have succeeded at almost any job he had decided to pursue. It is also difficult to imagine how he endured the years as a humble footslogger without resigning in frustration or being thrown out on his ear by outraged superiors, or how he ever achieved promotion to his present elevated rank. It is probable that in these days he had not yet acquired his later arrogance and was more prepared to conform and to turn that massive intellect to trivial and uninspiring tasks. Legend has it that one of his more perceptive superiors recognised his qualities and took the trouble to steer him gently through the troubled waters to his present safe and well-fitting niche. Stories abound of the sudden flashes of genius from him that illuminated the impenetrable dark of difficult cases, endearing him to the high and mighty and leading to his elevation but I doubt that his rise from the ranks happened that way at all and I strongly suspect that most of the examples quoted are apocryphal.

It says much for the Lothian and Borders Police that they are prepared to put up with a Chief Inspector who is bored by ninety percent of his job and, in consequence, is worse than useless at it, in order to have him available when the other ten percent appears on the scene. I suppose that it also says much for the squads whom he has commanded that they are also prepared to put up with him. Not that those at the bottom of the pile in any police force have much say in their fate. Though those of us who work under him often resent being landed with jobs he should be doing as well as our own, and spend a good deal of our time taking the mickey when he's at his most infuriating or arrogant, we would defend him to the death against any outsider. He has pulled too many chestnuts out of the fire for us in the past and, despite the appalling conceit of the man in assuming that we will be delighted to do, without a murmur of dissent, all the hard graft he should be tackling himself, we know that he has fought for us when we have got into trouble and always makes sure that we share in the credit when he has cracked one of the big ones. We have a real love-hate relationship with him but no-one has ever asked to be shifted from his squad.

As to me, I was born in Edinburgh and spent my early years in a tenement flat off Dundee Street. My father worked in a nearby brewery, of which Edinburgh at that time had more than its fair share, but he was killed in an accident at work when I was just eight years old. The firm did well by us according to their lights and the mores of the times. They gave the family a tiny pension and my mother a job serving food to the bosses in their canteen. As a result, we managed to live reasonably comfortable lives in comparison with many others in the area though money was always a bit on the tight side. And, since I was now the orphaned son of an Edinburgh burgess, I was eligible to became a Foundationer at George Heriot's School.

George Heriot, Jinglin' Geordie as Sir Walter Scott called him in his novel, was a goldsmith in the reign of James VI of Scotland. He made a pretty good living at his craft, but an even better one from lending money to the King and the courtiers who were always in need of a ready source of cash. When the sovereign became James 1 of the newly formed Great Britain and moved to London, Heriot went with him. Since the need for ready money was even greater there for a king and nobles living well beyond their means, Geordie found himself coining in the readies hand over fist. Since he had no heirs when he died, he left his money to found a school for the orphans of the Edinburgh citizenry.

The trustees were shrewd Scots businessmen who invested the money wisely. The Trust grew and prospered. More than a century ago the school expanded and opened its doors to all the sons of Edinburgh who could afford the fees, the Foundationers no longer boarding in the school building but receiving an allowance to stay elsewhere and attend the school, like the rest, as day pupils. I was one of these, staying at home with my mother during the night but mixing with the sons of the well-to-do middle classes on an equal footing during the day. I acquired not only a sound education but an insight into a life far removed from that of my mother. She had always been a great reader and from her I had acquired a love of literature. At Heriot's I added a liking for good music and the theatre. While I did well enough in exams, I was never one of the high flyers. Although I was urged by some of the teachers to go on to university and take a degree, I knew that wasn't for me. Book learning I had had enough of. I wanted some hands-on experience. I was keen to go on learning, but in the course of a job.

What led me to a career in the police I'm not sure. Perhaps it was the great respect for the law that my mother dinned into me. Or perhaps it was the lawlessness that I saw, and hated, in the jungle of tenements around where I lived. Since my mother refused point blank to leave the flat in which she had spent so much of her life and near which all her friends resided, and I didn't feel that I could desert her, my early years as a copper were not pleasant. My neighbours regarded me as a traitor to my roots and it was always uncomfortable when I was involved in any operation that impinged on the criminal occupations of the area. So, when my mother died, I moved as far away from the area as possible and bought a bungalow in Liberton on the southern side of the city. I still had the odd friend in the district where I'd grown up, but we tended to meet in town on the increasingly fewer occasions on which we got together. When you're in the police force and have come from a poor background, you have to make new friends to survive.

I got a transfer to the CID in due course and never looked back. Detective work proved to be my métier. I had a certain native intelligence and worked hard. I passed the sergeants' exams and got promoted. I hadn't been long a sergeant when I was informed that I was to be installed in Forsyth's squad, his previous sergeant having at last made it to the rank of Inspector, leaving a vacancy that had to be filled behind. I was initially flattered to be assigned to the team of a man with the kind of reputation that Forsyth had, since he was even then a bit of a legend, although I had heard that he could be a difficult man to work for. I soon found out that working for him was not likely to be a bed of roses and I was already somewhat disillusioned when the first murder case in which we were involved together came along. It was a pretty traumatic experience where the way in which Forsyth conducted the investigation almost gave me heart failure and where I feared at one time that my career in the police force was about to come to an ignominious end. I have chronicled these never to be forgotten events in a story entitled *The Crime Committee*. Fortunately, it turned out all right in the end and we became an established team.

These traumatic events that formed the beginning of our work as a team explain the odd relationship that I have with Forsyth. When you have seen Forsyth at his best and also at his worst, totally ignoring the rules of how a crime should be investigated, you find yourself a little short in the tugging of the forelock mentality.

CHAPTER 4

A couple of days after the murder of Murphy, at the end of the Wednesday, Forsyth went on holiday to one of the Greek islands. The team had plenty of tasks to keep it occupied and we had rather lost sight of the two murders that we had investigated when, on the following Monday, I was called to the office of the Chief Superintendent. I went there racking my brains to think of which sin that I had committed was likely to have got to the ear of authority. But when I knocked and entered after a curt command to do so, I found the Chief Super looking a trifle flustered and certainly not in the sort of mood that presaged a complete bollocking.

He gazed at me intently for a few minutes without saying anything and then, after a deep sigh, decided to take the plunge.

"It was Detective Chief Inspector Forsyth's team that looked into the deaths of two men who had been tortured before being murdered, wasn't it?"

Since he knew that perfectly well, the question was clearly rhetorical but I answered it in the affirmative none the less.

He gave a further sigh.

"I am not too happy to let you deal on your own with the new case involving torture and death that has just been reported to us," he said. "But you have the knowledge of whatever it was that Chief Inspector Forsyth made of the previous two cases and it seems sensible that you should look into the latest one. At least you can collect all the necessary evidence so that the Chief Inspector can deal with it all when he gets back. When is that happening, by the way?"

"He is off for a fortnight and has only been gone for five days."

He gave an even deeper sigh.

"Well, do the best that you can. I am sure that Forsyth will sort everything out when he returns."

With that ringing endorsement of the ability and competence of the four members of the Forsyth squad ringing in my ears, I went to alert the rest of the team to the fact that another case similar to the previous two had landed in our lap.

The attitude of the Chief Super had put my back up so much that I was determined to try to show him that we could solve cases even when Forsyth wasn't there. I found that the rest of the team felt much the same, although Beaumont and Fletcher were a trifle sceptical of our success, Jenkins, of course, supremely confident in his own ability, was in no doubt that his massive brain should be able to present the Chief Super with a triumphant solution.

The dead man had lived in the village of Pentafrick just south of Edinburgh. When we got there, we found that his Georgian stone house was on the edge of the village in a small acreage of well maintained ground. A few sightseers were hanging around the entrance to the garden but did nothing but goggle at me as I drove up to the gates. We had gone in two cars. I had Jenkins with me while the other two drove just behind. When we approached the gate, a uniform stopped us until we had established our identity and we then drove on and parked beside the house.

A uniformed sergeant was waiting for us at the front door. He informed me that the dead man was Oliver MacNair, who was the owner of the house. He had practised as a surveyor until recently when his father had died and left him not only the house but also a considerable sum of money. So MacNair had decided to retire from his occupation and live the life of a country gentleman. He was well liked in the village, took part in all the social activities and contributed generously to the local charities. The sergeant could think of no-one who would wish to harm him. The body had been found by the woman who came in to clean, a Mrs Graham. She was in the kitchen recovering from the shock of finding her employer in such a horrible condition.

I sent the other three off to nose about the village and find out what the local gossip was and went to have a look at the body. I found Dr Hay in the bedroom examining the body of a slim man in his mid-fifties with a mop of ginger hair who was strapped to a chair, with cigarette burns and cuts all over his naked body. His haggard face showed evidence of the pain he had suffered before death had supervened. Hay saw me as I entered the room and moved over to greet me, at the same time removing his cigar case from his pocket and extracting a cheroot from it. Having lit this and enjoyed a lungful of the resultant smoke, he was prepared to talk to me.

"I hear that Forsyth is on holiday," he said. "I didn't think that they let you out on your own."

I ignored the sally.

"Since we handled the last two cases," I pointed out, "they had little option. But, of course, they expect us to be completely flummoxed and to have to wait until the Chief gets back."

"Show the bastards that they wrong you," he said. "It is time that that lot stopped believing that only the Inspectors have brains. Show them that the foot soldiers can have inspirations as well."

"We will certainly try to do that," I told him. "Can you

give us a head start? Is there anything new or of interest about this case?"

He sucked in another lungful of smoke before making a reply.

"It is exactly the same as the last two," he said as he blew smoke out from his mouth. "Totally unnecessary sadism with the victim pegging out before the killer was able to get what he wanted. He must get a lot of pleasure from inflicting pain. But he would do a hell of a lot better to be more delicate in the way he inflicts the torture. That way he could keep them going for longer and have more chance of getting whatever information it is that he so desperately wants."

Hay left and I learned that the forensics man had found nothing of interest. I had a word with the uniformed sergeant who knew all about the village and who informed me that the dead man's best friend in the village was a Basil Henderson, who had retired early from a job in a bank when his wife had died. He also said that that the minister, Andrew Constable, kept his ear to the ground and knew everything that went on in the local area and that a woman called Sybil Arbuthnot was the person who knew everyone and gathered up all the local gossip. I determined that I would deal with these three and was sure that the others would tour the village and surrounding houses and find out from the rest of the population whatever else was worth knowing.

Basil Henderson lived in a large, well furnished cottage in the middle of the village. He was a sturdy figure with a red face and thinning grey hair and dressed in expensive tweeds. He was happy to be interviewed by me but seemed in a state of shock from what had happened to his friend. He said that he badly needed a scotch to help him to get back to normality and offered me one as well. Although it was a little early in the day for me, I decided to accept the offer.

Once he had poured the drinks, we sat down in comfortable chairs. I took a sip of the whisky and found that it was one of the well known blends. I suppose that not everyone is into malts. Not everyone has a knowledgeable Forsyth available to guide him through the mysteries of the whisky trade.

"I can't imagine anyone wanting to do those awful things to anyone," Henderson told me after he had swallowed a large draught of whisky, "far less Oliver, who was the sweetest, kindest man alive."

"Have you known Mr MacNair for a long time?" I asked.

"We were at school together. We drifted apart a bit after that as our paths diverged during our working lives but we kept in touch over the years and, when he moved back here after his father died and left everything to him, we renewed our friendship. He was a solitary man who didn't have all that many intimate friends but I am happy to say that I was one of them."

"And has he ever suggested at any time that he was fearful that something dreadful like this might happen to him?"

"Never. He hadn't a care in the world as far as I could see."

"So he had no enemies who might wish him harm that you were aware of?"

"None at all," he insisted forcefully. "And he didn't mix with the sort of person who would do these terrible things to him."

"Did he ever mention the names of Norman Mathers or Tom Murphy?"

We had kept out of the press the fact that the two previous victims had been tortured. We like to keep something up our sleeves so that we can weed out the crank calls that flood in from weirdos who come out of the woodwork after every murder. So there was no reason why Henderson would connect their deaths to that of his friend, even if he remembered the names from the newspaper accounts.

Henderson thought about it briefly before shaking his head.

"I don't remember him mentioning either name. Have they anything to do with this crime?"

"It was just a random thought that had occurred to me," I said untruthfully. "When was the last time you saw him?"

"Yesterday afternoon."

"And did he seem at all agitated or was he looking ill at ease?"

"He seemed the same as he always was. Perfectly happy and contented with his lot."

"Had he an interest in either the theatre or in football?" I enquired.

"We very occasionally took in a show, mainly musicals," he replied. "And he wasn't a football man. Rugby was his thing."

So there seemed to be no connection between MacNair and the other two and I left the cottage shortly thereafter.

I found the minister in the church which was one of the oldest in the area, though it looked as if it needed a good deal of repairs done to it. Indeed there was a poster by the gate seeking contributions to a restoration fund. Presumably money was not in too great a supply in the local presbytery. The Reverend Andrew Constable was a tall, ascetic man clad in a black suit with a prominent dog collar. He looked to be in sombre mood, the death of one of his more prominent parishioners hanging heavily on his mind. He expressed himself as happy to answer any of my questions.

"Oliver was a real Christian gentleman," he told me. "He was a regular attender at our services and gave generously to all the causes that were raised in the village. He was also a man who didn't hold grudges but forgave his enemies."

I fastened on the last bit.

"So he did have enemies?"

"Not any who would do these dreadful things to him. I was referring to the petty jealousies that one comes across in a village like this one."

"Maybe you are not as familiar with the other people in the village as you imagine," I suggested. "Perhaps one of them has a secret side that only appeared last night after he had brooded for some time one one of these petty jealousies."

He dismissed the suggestion with a negligent wave of his hand.

"Believe me," he said. "I know my parishioners well enough to be certain that none of them would treat anyone, far less Oliver, in the way that injury was inflicted on MacNair last night."

"Has he ever mentioned in conversation with you," I asked, "the names of either a Norman Mathers or a Tom Murphy?"

Constable thought for a few seconds.

"I am sure that I have heard both of these names somewhere, but in what context I cannot recall. But I am sure that neither has ever been been mentioned to me by Oliver."

"And did he make trips to Edinburgh from time to time?"

"Only very occasionally. He loved the village and seldom left it. And, when he did make a trip to the city, it was usually in the company of one or more of the people from the village."

Sybil Arbuthnot had apparently been the leader of all things in the village until MacNair had retired there. She was a tall, angular lady with a loud voice and decisive gestures. I got the impression immediately that MacNair had not been her dearest friend.

"He was the sort of person," she informed me, "who courts popularity by being all things to all men. He enjoyed a certain respect in consequence. But the fate that has befallen him now would appear to indicate that he mixed with some very odd characters indeed."

"Have you ever come across instances before that he might have among his acquaintances some who were peculiar?" I asked.

"No," she admitted reluctantly. "But he had enough sense to keep that side of his activities well hidden from the rest of us in the village."

"Have you ever heard him mention the names of either Norman Mathers or Tom Murphy?" I enquired.

"Are these two members of the criminal fraternity with whom McNair was known to have contact?" she asked excitedly.

"I am afraid that I am not at liberty to give the source of any information that the police may possess," I said sanctimoniously.

"I can understand that," she replied. "No, I have never heard either name mentioned."

There seemed no point in continuing the conversation with her, since she had clearly a jaundiced view of McNair. So I returned to the crime scene, made arrangements for everything to be taken care of and returned to Fettes. There I wrote up a full report for the Chief Super, delivered it to his office, taking good care to give it to his secretary and get out of sight before he could grab me.

I spent the rest of the time setting up an incident room to deal with the latest crime. By the time that five o'clock came round, I had done a very full day's work and was feeling in need of a rest. I therefore made my way to the pub in which we did our drinking.

When I got there, I found that the rest of the team were already in residence. I got myself a pint of heavy at the bar counter, lighting up a cigarette as I waited for the order to be fulfilled and then joined the others. After having a large swallow of the liquid from my glass, I was ready to start the evening's proceedings.

I began, as usual, by telling them everything that I had learned that day. When I had finished, I had another swallow of beer and invited them to enlighten the rest of us with what they had achieved. They had between them talked to everyone in the village and the surrounding area. The story from all of them was the same. MacNair had been well liked. A few of the residents, like Sybil Arbuthnot, thought that he was on the pushy, lord of the manor, side and taking too much on to himself. But even they were mystified as to how MacNair could be mixed up with people who would torture and kill their fellow human beings. Even the most critical of his fellows found it difficult to associate him with such people.

At the end of the recitals, I gave a sigh.

"We are getting absolutely nowhere with these investigations," I pointed out. "And we will continue to get nowhere until we find out what is the connection between these people. So what you lot will be doing tomorrow is going with a fine tooth-comb through the lives of these three people. Andy will take Mathers, Sid will concentrate on Murphy and Martin will investigate MacNair. Go from the cradle to the grave with each of them. And, if you come across anything that looks at all interesting, see if it applies to the others as well. I will try to keep the Chief Super off our backs and I will also be thinking of any connection that might be worth exploring."

And there it was left. We had another round of drinks together and then Jenkins and I left. The other two ordered food from the bar and settled in for another evening together.

Anna arrived later that evening. She had been racking her brains throughout the day to find a connection between Mathers and Murphy and had learned from the BBC news of the death of MacNair and had put two and two together and correctly arrived at four.

"The only way that people like an accountant, a labourer, and a lord of the manor can have a connection," she said confidently, "is through one of these secret male chauvinist organisations like the masons. The toffs let in folk from the working classes in order to have people to do all the hard chores for them."

"I don't think that that is quite how it works in these organisations," I suggested. "Not that I have any first hand experience."

"But you take my point that it is in that sort of society that people from different classes meet."

"I do," I assured her. "And I think that it shows the incisiveness of your mind that you came up with the suggestion. Unfortunately, I have to tell you that I also thought of that and checked it out. Neither Mathers nor Murphy, as far as I could determine, was a member of any such organisation."

She was a trifle disappointed that her bright suggestion had not cracked the case but soon brightened up as we went upstairs and took part in some interesting activities in bed.

CHAPTER 5

It was on the following day when I was writing up a report in the office that I share with three other sergeants when the door opened and Fletcher came in. I looked up and gathered from the expression on his face what it was that he was going to tell me.

"I have found out," he said, "what connects these three dead people."

"Well done. So what is it links the three together?" I asked.

But Sid was not going to have his moment of glory finish so quickly.

"In our discussion," he reminded me, "we thought that one of the few ways that people from different backgrounds could be related was through membership of an organisation like the masons."

He paused dramatically.

I nodded and waited.

"But it struck me today, as I was turning it over in my mind, that there is another way that we hadn't thought of, and these people are all of the right age for it. Disparate people get stuck together when they are in the armed forces."

"So you think that they may have served together in one of the Services during the course o f the Second World

War?"

"I not only think it. I have verified that they did," he said complacently.

As I said earlier, Fletcher is not the brightest of the team, but he startles us from time to time by coming up with the brightest of ideas.

"Very well thought out," I said. "Which service were they all in? Was it the army, navy or the air force they served?"

"They were all in the Army. They were in the Black Watch in fact. I checked that that was true with friends of each of them."

"Why didn't this come up before?" I pondered. "They must have met at reunions. Why didn't anyone mention this to us?"

"Mathers was only in the Army for a year or so. And he hated every minute of it. So, when he was demobbed, he never had any contact with the Army again. No visits to reunions."

"And Murphy?"

"He attended a couple of reunions just after the end of the war. But his life was not such that he kept that up and he hasn't had anything to do with his Army colleagues recently."

"But I imagine that MacNair went to all the reunions," I

suggested.

"You're right," he replied. "But, since the other two weren't going, their names were never mentioned to anyone by MacNair."

I congratulated Fletcher again on an inspired thought and he went off looking very pleased with himself, as he had every right to be.

I rang up the Black Watch Museum in Perth and spoke to a Colonel Rutherford, who was in charge. I explained to him the sort of information that I was hoping that he could provide for me and arranged to visit him on the following day.

The next morning I drove in bright sunshine through to Perth and visited the Museum. Rutherford turned out to be an elderly silver-haired man with an upright carriage, very correctly dressed in a discreet suit, white shirt and regimental tie.

"Did you find out anything about the three men who were murdered?" I asked after the preliminary greetings were out of the way.

'I have," he replied. "They were all in the 9th Battalion which was part of the 51st Highland Division during the Second World War."

"And did they serve in the same unit together at any

time?"

"The only time that the three served together was around the time of the Ardennes Offensive, also known as the Battle of the Bulge."

"I've heard about that,' I said. "It was a German offensive towards the end of the war."

"That is correct."

"But the Germans were being pushed back and on the run at that time. What did they hope to achieve by going on the offensive?"

"Their objective was to capture Antwerp," he told me. "Since this was a main hub for the supplying of the Allied Armies at that time, the disruption that would have been caused would have had a devastating effect on the conduct of the war."

"But did they have a real chance of capturing Antwerp?" I quizzed.

"Their aim was also to burst through a weak point on the Allied front in the Ardennes," he explained, "and to encircle and annihilate the armies on either side. Had that succeeded, they might well have gone on and captured Antwerp. And they believed that they would then have been in a position to negotiate an end to the war in the West which would have allowed them to concentrate on winning the war in the east."

"But surely," I said, "the Allies would have been able to see the enormous build-up of forces behind the enemy lines?"

"Unfortunately not. Due to a combination of arrogance, a belief that the Germans would be unable to mount a major offensive, a concentration on their own plans and poor air reconnaissance, the Americans didn't see what was coming. They even ignored some warnings that they did get that something was going on behind the German lines."

"So the Americans were taken completely by surprise by the German attack?"

"They were," he agreed. "The Germans did break through the Ardennes front which was rather poorly defended. It was a total shambles. The American High Command had little idea of what was going on. The American forces that survived were fighting in the dark in units with little communication between themselves or headquarters."

"So how did the Allied forces manage to stop the Germans from annihilating two armies and getting to Antwerp?" I asked.

"Eisenhower put the British commander, General Montgomery, in charge of the situation," the Colonel explained.

"But the American commanders didn't like Montgomery one little bit," I pointed out. "They must have just loved that."

"They hated it. They thought him too bumptious and far too cautious. But caution was just what was needed at that time. And, of course, for Montgomery it was a dream come true. It is said that he arrived at the American Headquarters like Christ come to cleanse the Temple. And he didn't make his move until he had all units in touch with him and with one another. Then he counter-attacked and saved the situation."

"It is all very interesting," I told him. "But what has this to do with what I am trying to find out about the three men who were murdered?"

"They were among the British troops," he explained, "who were sent into battle to restore the situation in the Ardennes. And their unit was caught in a counter-attack by the Germans and badly mauled. The platoon which held the three men in whom you are interested got isolated from the rest of the battalion and also lost several of its members. So a second lieutenant and ten men found themselves completely isolated and lost behind the enemy lines. It took them three very difficult and dangerous days involving further losses of personnel, to get back to the Allied positions."

"And this was the only time that these three were in action together?" I asked.

"It was the only time that they were in the same unit together. When they had had time to recover from their ordeal, they were split up and sent to reinforce different battalions."

I thought for a time about what the colonel had told me. If this was the only time that the three had served together, what information could the killer possibly be looking for when he was torturing the surviving members of the platoon.

"Is there any chance," I asked, "that one of the platoon let the others down in some way while they were lost behind the enemy lines and that one of the survivors is seeking revenge for a comrade who was lost becase of the action?"

He thought about it for a while.

"It's a possibility," he said. "But why would he leave it for so long before doing anything about it? It doesn't really make sense."

"Perhaps a member of the family of one of the dead has only recently heard that it was the action of one of the platoon that caused the death."

"So why is he going after so many of the platoon? They couldn't all have been doing things that let the dead man down."

"I suppose you are right," I said. "And, if a family member is involved, it would take a major effort to go through all the possible people who could be suspects. Let's see if we can find a reason for the deaths among the survivors of the platoon."

An interesting idea had began to form in my brain and I considered it carefully for a time before turning back to the Colonel.

"Is it possible," I asked, "that, in the three days that they were behind enemy lines, they could have stumbled across something like gold or diamonds that the Nazi High Command had stolen from Jews or other of the peoples whom they had conquered?"

He looked at me a trifle askance but, after some thought, he nodded his head and answered me in the affirmative.

"I see what your reasoning is. And it is quite possible that that could be the case. By that stage of the war, several of the Nazis in the higher command were convinced that they were going to finish on the losing side and were already making preparations for a comfortable old age in South America. One of these people might have thought that the Ardennes Offensive provided him with an excellent opportunity to get some of the more valuable stuff that he had looted out of the country via a liberated Antwerp."

"And, if our heroes," I said thoughtfully, "unexpectedly came across the group that was carrying the stuff, had to engage with them, killed them and then discovered what they had been carrying, they might have decided to bury it secretly with the intention of going back after the war was finished. The looted items would have provided them with a very nice stake to set them up for the peace that was to follow."

He thought about my suggestion for a few minutes before commenting.

"Then why did they never go back to get it?" he demanded.

"Maybe they did," I suggested. "But, if the area was fought over fiercely after they had left the scene, the markers that they had left in order to be able to recover the loot might well have been blown away to kingdom come. And, although they searched for it, they may never have found it."

He gave consideration to my suggestion for a few seconds.

"That would be not unlikely. And you believe that someone is now trying to find out what he can about the affair so that he can have a go at finding the treasure himself?"

"It is certainly one possibility as I see it," I agreed. "But what I need to know from you is who else was in that platoon that was lost behind enemy lines and how many of them are still alive. Because, whatever it was that happened all these years ago, one of them must be involved in some way with the deaths we have been investigating."

"I thought that you might wish to talk to any survivors from that time," he said., "so I looked into that. The lieutenant is still alive. His name is George Menzies and he lives on an estate just south of Edinburgh. He comes to all the reunions. Of the ten men who found themselves behind the lines, two were killed as they made their way back to safety. Two more have died of natural causes since the end of the war. Two have emigrated, one to Australia and one to Canada. The remaining man is a Graham Mellor. He still lives in Edinburgh. I have already written out for you the addresses of the two men in whom you were likely to have an interest."

I took the paper that the Colonel offered and thanked him for his help. I offered to buy him a drink, which he refused, and I suggested that, if he ever felt in need of refreshment when he was in Edinburgh, that he should give me a ring. I returned to the car and made the return journey to the capital.

CHAPTER 6

I had made arrangements to visit George Menzies the next day and set off from Fettes about ten. It was a pleasant drive from the centre of Edinburgh along the A7 towards the Borders. Menzies stayed with his wife near Gorebridge in a quite large three-storeyed house in the middle of an estate that he had inherited when his father had died.

He turned out to be a man in his early sixties, still looking healthy and active, with a lean face and silver hair, and dressed in slacks and an open necked shirt. His wife, Pamela, was smaller but also looked like an outdoor type and had obviously once been quite a beauty. I found out that also staying with them was a younger brother called Geoffrey who had gone off before I arrived and a son, Peter, who was out playing golf. I was offered coffee, which I gratefully accepted, and Pamela went off to the kitchen to make it.

"You want to ask me about some of the men who served under me during the war, you said on the phone," said Menzies.

"Three people have been murdered in the Edinburgh area recently," I explained, "and the only connection between them that we could find was that they all served in a platoon under your command at about the time of the

Battle of the Bulge."

"What were the names of the men involved?" he asked.

"A Norman Mathers, a Tom Murphy and an Oliver MacNair."

"I remember the three of them," he said. "We had a pretty hairy time together during the Ardennes Offensive and were lucky to get out alive. So one doesn't forget those who have shared that sort of life or death experience with you. I haven't seen Mathers or Murphy recently but I have run across MacNair from time to time at Black Watch reunions."

"The three men were all tortured before being killed," I told him. "That is something about which we have kept very quiet and I would ask you not to pass that information on to anyone else. It looked as if the killer was trying to obtain from them some valuable knowledge that they all possessed. Have you any idea what that might have been?"

"Not a clue. But then I haven't seen two of them for years. I would not know what they had got up to in the years since the end of the war."

"We are pretty certain that they had not got together since they parted after the Ardennes Offensive ended. So it looks as if whatever information they held was obtained at the time that they were serving together under your command."

He looked utterly surprised.

"Then I am completely at a loss to understand what the killer would have been looking for."

The wife returned with coffee and chocolate biscuits, so that I had to stop the questioning until we had all been served. Menzies explained to his wife what it was that I had been enquiring about.

"You didn't, during the time that you were behind the enemy lines, come across, for example, some Nazi loot?" I asked.

He looked a trifle startled at first and then gave a laugh.

"That sounds like the plot of a rather far fetched Hollywood movie," he suggested, "involving Clint Eastwood or some similar star."

"I gather that quite a few of the troops in the second World War came across Nazi loot and held on to it or buried it to go back to it after hostilities had ended. So it is not just fiction."

"And he thinks that you and your men might also might have been involved in such clandestine activities," suggested his wife.

"One has to consider all the possibilities," I pointed

out.

"So, if we had done what you are suggesting," he said, "why hasn't whatever it was we buried been uncovered long ago and been shared out and disposed of?"

"If the area got heavily bombed after you had left it," I suggested, "you might have found it difficult to recognise the particular location where you had deposited the loot you had found."

"If that were so," he enquired, "who would now be interested in finding at this late date where the loot was deposited?"

"I hoped that you would be able to point me in that direction."

"Since the whole thing is nothing but fantasy, I am afraid that I am not in a position to help you," he said with great emphasis.

And there I had to leave it. We parted amicably enough but I could feel that he was not unhappy to see me go. But whether this was because he was keen to be shot of a man who thought incorrectly that he had been involved in illegal activities or whether I had got too close to the truth for comfort it was hard to tell.

I also paid a visit to Graham Mellor. I had made a few enquiries about him beforehand and had been told that he had for some time run a successful butcher's business, having owned three shops in the Edinburgh area. But I had also been informed that it was believed that he was behind some of the crime in the region. He was thought to be the financier behind some of the more spectacular and successful ram raids that had taken place in the city. He didn't get involved in the raids himself. He merely financed these operations and then took a large cut of the proceedings.

Mellor lived in an expensive house in the Braid Hills area of the city and was a prominent member of one of the local golf clubs. He turned out to be a heavy set man with a round, red face, luxuriant wavy black hair and a charming manner. He was dressed in casual clothes that must have cost him a pretty penny, was smoking a large cigar and drinking from a glass that contained twenty-year-old malt whisky. I know this because he told me what it was when he offered me some of the same. But I felt that I had to decline, being on duty, and the offer coming from a member of the criminal fraternity.

"And to what do I owe the pleasure of this visit?" he asked me with a smile.

"You were in the Black Watch during the Second World War," I suggested.

He seemed a trifle taken aback. I got the impression

that he had expected the police to be visiting him for some totally different reason.

"I was," he said guardedly.

"And you were a member of a platoon that unfortunately got stuck behind the enemy lines during the Battle of the Bulge."

"I was," he agreed. "And a very unpleasant time was had by all. But why on earth would that be of interest to the police at this time?"

"Three other members of that platoon have recently been murdered and the only thing that they had in common was belonging to that platoon."

"But why would anyone want to kill these people after all this time?" he enquired.

"I was hoping that you might be able to provide some reason for these deaths occurring."

"I noticed in the paper that MacNair had been murdered," he said. "Who were the other ones who were killed?"

"Norman Mathers and Tom Murphy."

"I remember them all right. You remember people with whom you have gone through a very soul-searing experience. But I don't think that I have come across either of them since the war ended. MacNair I meet from time to time at Black Watch reunions. But I don't know any of them well enough to hazard a guess as to why someone would want to kill them."

"We believe that the reason for the killings lies in what happened all these years ago in the Ardennes," I told him.

"You think that some oddball German son has been holding a grudge against us because we killed his father in the war all these years ago?" he said sceptically. "That's just rubbish."

"It has been suggested that you may have come across some Nazi loot while you were behind the lines. And that you buried it for collection when it was safe to do so after the war."

"But, even if that were true, which it isn't, that was over thirty years ago. Why would anybody be doing anything about it now?"

"If one of you ripped off the others, someone might have recently got wind of what had been done and be looking for compensation."

"Since we found and buried no loot at any time," he said dogmatically, "you are barking up the wrong tree. So whoever is killing these people, it has nothing to do with me."

And there I had to leave it.

That evening, the team met as usual in the pub.

Fletcher bought a round and, after we had sampled it, I gave them all the scant information that I had obtained from Menzies and Mellor. They already knew all that I had learned from the Colonel who looked after the Black Watch Museum.

"Do you think that Menzies was telling you the whole truth?" asked Jenkins.

"It is very difficult to tell," I said. "He could well be lying. And it is even more difficult to see why the three men were tortured and killed unless the murderer was trying to find out about something of value which he believes exists and was discovered by that lost platoon during the Battle of the Bulge."

"Is it possible that Menzies has long since liberated whatever it was that they found without telling the others?" asked Beaumont.

"He seemed to be living quite comfortably," I replied, "and he was able to retire early. But he was not showing ostentatiously that he was wealthy."

"But, if he had any sense," Fletcher pointed out, "he wouldn't flash around any wealth that he had acquired in that way in case the other members of the platoon became suspicious of how exactly he had acquired so great an amount of cash."

"There is that," I agreed.

"And what about Mellor?" asked Fletcher.

"He is almost certainly into providing the funding for crime. And it is possible that that money came from the loot hidden away during the war. But he is also the sort that would want revenge if he thought that he had been done out of his share of the Nazi loot. So I could see him stopping at nothing to get at the truth. But whether he actually did or not is another matter altogether."

"So what do we do now?" asked Beaumont.

"I don't think that there is much we can do about Mellor at this point apart from finding out if he has alibis for any of the times when one of the others was being tortured and killed. I will look into that. The rest of you can try to find out whether Menzies did the dirty on the others over the Nazi loot. So we do a blanket job on him. We find out what his profession was after he came out of the Army, whether his wife had money, how much he has in the bank, what his investments are. And we try to find out whether he has more money to his name than can be accounted for by what he has earned by the sweat of his brow. Or that he has been lucky enough to inherit from his wife or his parents."

And I preceded to share out the tasks that such a survey would entail.

We met again in the pub the following evening having

all been out all day finding out what we could about Menzies and Mellor. Beaumont supplied the first round and offered cigarettes to Sid and me. After we had all slaked our thirst, and the smokers had had a few puffs to absorb some nicotine, I started the ball rolling by telling them what I had found out.

"As far as I could discover," I said, "Mellor could have done all the killings of the other members of the platoon. On two of the occasions, he was allegedly on his own at home. And, unless he had a woman in for the night, he has no alibi. On the third occasion he was supposed to be at his golf club at a boozy do they were holding that went on into the wee small hours. But there was a period when he was not seen by anyone for quite some time. He has a reputation as a bit of a ladies' man and might have been indulging in a little dalliance. But he could also have spent the missing time slipping off and doing the torturing and killing of his former fellow soldier."

They absorbed this information and then Beaumont took up the story.

"Menzies comes from a fairly wealthy family," he told us, "which for ages has owned a lot of the land around Gorebridge. The estate is entailed and has to go to the eldest son. So he inherited the estate when his father died. But his father had allowed the estate to run down badly, being more interested in women and gambling than in making sure that the family and its fortunes prospered. But the estate is now doing very well. The new man in charge has managed to turn things around. But whether this was done solely by hard work on his part or whether an injection of cash from illegally acquired goodies was a contributing factor, it is difficult to say. And we wouldn't be able to determine what caused the improvement without getting a look at the books over the last few years."

"And you are never going to get a court order to do that on the slim evidence of possible wrongdoing that we possess," suggested Jenkins.

"You are absolutely correct," I informed him. "So we are for the moment completely stymied. How did you get on in chatting to the natives, Sid?"

"The locals like him well enough," Fletcher conceded. "Getting the estate back to its working best has provided a number of jobs for the area, so they are grateful to him for that. And he has given support, including financial help, to quite a few local activities. But the family doesn't mix much with the locals, so they are regarded as a bit on the snooty side, particularly the wife and the brother. And the son is apparently an arrogant little sod who expects the local peasantry to do whatever he wants them to without question."

He paused to have another refreshing drink of his beer.

"But nobody," he continued, once he had slaked his thirst, "has seen any evidence of conspicuous consumption on the part of Menzies or his family. So, if he picked up the loot from the continent without telling the others, he has had the sense not to make it obvious that he has come into wealth."

He sat back and took a large swallow of beer. I looked over expectantly at Jenkins. He, in his turn, had a swig from his gin and tonic before giving us the benefit of his findings.

"His income tax returns," he said, "don't show any abnormal amounts of money having been acquired over the last few years. And he hasn't got large amounts of money going into or coming from his bank accounts. In other words, he doesn't appear to have more cash around than one would expect from his earnings from the estate. But he would be unlikely to deposit any loot he had acquired illegally in an obvious place like a bank account or put too much money on display at any time."

He stopped and took another small sample of his gin and tonic.

"And he may, of course, have investments tucked away in some tax haven," he went on, "that we have no access to. But the investments that he is known to possess are not more than you would expect for a man who has successfully turned round a failing estate into a prosperous one."

"So, if he did do the dirty on his men after the war," I said thoughtfully, "he has been careful to give no hint of it to them or to anyone else. And the person who is killing off the platoon members clearly does not have any notion that Menzies may have helped himself quietly to the money or he wouldn't be bothering spending his time torturing the men. He would be screwing the necessary information from the lieutenant."

"So do we think that it is Mellor who is killing off the other members of the platoon because he has got a hint that one of them helped himself to the loot that they had stashed away?" asked Fletcher.

"He is the only one who seems to have the right motive," I pointed out. "And he fits the profile of the person who is doing the killing. We have to go with him unless anyone has a better idea."

But nobody had. We tossed it backwards and forwards a bit more but got nowhere. We had another round before Jenkins and I left but it was ob vious that we had no clear idea as to how to proceed.

I was greeted at my house in Liberton by an Anna in

the process of producing the evening meal. She seemed to be bursting to share with me some interesting thought but had enough sense to wait before saying anything until we were consuming the last of the wine that we had had with the dinner. I let her know how the case was progressing. She listened with care to the account of our conversation in the pub and then asked the first question.

"Are you happy with the notion that it is Mellor who is behind all the killings?"

"I am not," I said. "Unfortunately, I don't see any alternative. But there are a few problems about it being Mellor who is killing off the others. Why would he go after Mathers and Murphy first when it should have been obvious that, if any of them had helped themselves to the loot, the only ones who showed the slightest signs of wealth at all were Menzies and MacNair? Why had he not gone and had a go at these two more likely suspects immediately?"

She pondered that for a while and then let me know what had been on her mind all along.

"I think that you are looking in totally the wrong direction," she said.

"So what other direction is there in which to have a look?"

She had become quite animated.

"You have found no evidence that any of them

possess more money than would normally be expected, have you?"

I conceded that we hadn't.

"And it takes a bit of a stretch of the imagination to think of how any of them, at this late date, would get the notion that they had been done out of their share of the buried loot."

I agreed that that also was unlikely.

"But where do these interesting questions take us?" I asked.

"After all this time," she suggested, "it is not unlikely that one of them would confess to someone whom they considered to be a friend that they had buried Nazi loot on the continent during the war but couldn't later find it because the area had been severely fought over and shelled."

"I will grant you that, but so what?"

"If the loot consisted of bars of gold or silver, that friend might realise that, although the platoon had been unable thirty years ago to find the treasure, he now might be able to do so. If he went to the area with a metal detector, he might well be able to find the location of the illegally obtained loot."

I thought about it for a few minutes. It made a lot of sense.

"And, after all these years, the memory of where the loot had been buried might well be a bit dim in the minds of the people involved," I said. "And they might have been tortured to death not because they were withholding the information from the killer but because their memories was somewhat faulty."

"I think that that makes more sense than that Mellor is killing off his former mates."

"It certainly opens up a new and interesting line of investigation," I said thoughtfully. Then I gave a sigh. "But how do we find the putative greedy friend. It might be anyone?"

"Since Mathers was the first one to be tortured," she suggested, "isn't it likely that he was the one who was indiscreet enough to mention the loot? And, while he was being tortured, he would have revealed the names of the others who had been in the platoon."

"We can certainly start with him. And, since he didn't have all that many friends, it shouldn't be too difficult to find out to which of them he would be likely to reveal such a secret. We will start with his best friend, John Summers, and see where that gets us. And, if we draw a blank with Mathers' few buddies, we can go on to those who knew Murphy, starting with the fellow with whom he went to football matches at Easter Road and elsewhere, Desmond

Bannon. And MacNair had a friend called Basil Henderson to whom he might have confessed what the platoon had got up to during the war. Since there are the buddies of three men to be investigated, I will give one of them to each of the team to look into."

I leered over at Anna.

"And, as a reward for coming up with that bright idea, I shall now take you upstairs and give you the most interesting experience of our life."

CHAPTER 7

We worked all Saturday and had a session in the pub that night. I supplied the first round and allowed them to have a few drinks of the satisfying liquid before asking them to report. Beaumont started the ball rolling.

"I am not sure what you expected us to find out," he told me. "I think that your idea that it is someone not connected with the original platoon who is doing all this is a sound one. It explains a lot that puzzled us when we thought that one of the old soldiers was involved. But we interviewed all these people who might have heard of the loot from one of the platoon and none of them seemed the type to torture and kill their fellows. And I am not sure that our investigating them again will yield anything. The culprit will not have the mark of Cain on his forehead and it could take us months to get even a sniff of who is a likely candidate."

You will see that I had given them the impression that the idea about the outsider being responsible for the killings had come from me. I was not trying to steal Anna's glory. But it would not be a good idea if it were known that I discussed ongoing cases with someone who was not connected with the police.

"I know that it is a hard and unrewarding slog," I assured him, "and one that may not realise any results in the short term. But we have to follow up the lead to see if we can get a notion of who is involved."

But none of them had got a glimmer of who might have found out about the loot and, although they said that they would continue to look into possible candidates, it was obvious that all of them thought that they were on a wild goose chase.

"I had a word with both Menzies and Mellor," I told them. "I suggested that they might both be at risk from the person who had killed their former comrades. I even suggested that they might like to have someone from the police staying in their houses with them. Both pooh-poohed the idea that they might be in danger and said that they could handle successfully by themselves any problems that might arise. I don't think that we can do any more than that."

They agreed and we went on to discuss other matters not connected with the case.

It was three days later that I got the call from Sergeant Anderson that informed me that George Menzies had been found murdered in the grounds of his estate. I alerted the team to the latest news and we proceeded to the murder scene in two cars.

When we got to the Gorebridge estate, I added my car to the many that were already parked outside the house. I sent Andy Beaumont to find out from the locals what he could about the circumstances of the death and to organise the others in whatever duties he thought necessary and went off to the area of the grounds in which the body had been found.

When I got to the murder scene, I found a local uniformed sergeant standing leaning against a tree and watching Dr Hay at work. The latter was just getting up from the dead body of Menzies as I approached, at the same time fumbling in his pocket for his cigar case. Once he had opened this, extracted from it one of his evil-smelling cheroots and lit it, he was prepared to give me his full attention.

"We don't seem to be getting anywhere with this lot of murders, do we?" he said. "They still keep happening. Of course, there's a difference this time. The poor fellow managed to get away and make a run for it. Not that it did him much good. The killer still caught up with him and finished off the job."

I looked down at the body of Menzies as it lay on the ground. He lay face down and he was naked and had the usual cuts and burns to which I had become accustomed on his body. Menzies had a gag in his mouth and his hands were tied together in front of his body. There were marks on his legs where cords had been but there were none in evidence now. A cheap knife, of the kind that could be bought in every hardware shop in the country, protruded from his back.

I turned to the sergeant.

"What's your assessment of what happened here?" I asked.

"It looks as if someone broke into the house during the night," he replied. "There's a window forced round the back. Mr Menzies was hit over the head while he slept and then carried out into the garden. He was tied to a tree nearer to the house than this place, with a gag in his mouth."

"Wasn't his wife wakened by him being carted out of the bedroom?"

"They occupy separate bedrooms. He apparently snores badly enough to wake the dead. So he sleeps in a different room from her."

"And how did he finish up here?"

"The killer must have left him alone while he did something else. And it looks as if he hadn't been tied to the tree securely enough so that he was able to break free. He managed to get the cord off his legs so that he could run away. You can follow his path as he crashed through the shrubbery in the dark. But the killer would have been able to hear his progress as well, caught up with him and finished him off."

I signalled to a nearby forensic man.

"Can you check the handle of the knife for fingerprints," I asked.

He busied himself at the task and then looked up at me and shook his head.

"It's been wiped clean or, more likely, he was wearing gloves."

"When did all these interesting happenings occur?" I asked Dr Hay.

"He died around the two o'clock mark this morning," was the answer that I got. "There's also something that might be of interest to you. The stab from the knife that killed him was almost certainly made by a person who is left-handed."

"That is something that might well be of great use," I said. "Thank you."

Hay departed and I followed the trail back through the shrubbery that Menzies had made till I got to the tree where he had initially been tied. There were scuff marks on the trunk and the length of cord that had at one time been around Menzies' ankles lay not far away. A short distance from the tree I came across a muddy area where there was the print of a man's left shoe that had been used to press a cigarette end into the earth and put it out. I dropped to my knees and examined the mark and came to the conclusion that it was a size ten shoe that had made the impression in the mud. I gave instructions that a cast of the mark should be made.

I had a further look around the grounds but found nothing else of interest and so proceeded back into the house. I went first to the bedroom that Menzies had occupied and from which he had been abducted and had a good look at its contents. It was a well and expensively furnished room with a deep pile carpet, a king sized bed, a wardrobe, a dressing table and an occasional table by the bedside that held an alarm clock, a watch, a lamp and a glass that contained a small quantity of a fruit drink. Attached to the bedroom was a bathroom which had all the usual offices. I examined both rooms with great thoroughness. I noted that Menzies' shoes had all been size ten.

While I was examining the space underneath the bed, my eye was caught by a glint from something that was almost completely concealed by one of the legs of the bed. I poked around with a pen and drew it out from its concealment. It turned out to be a cuff link with the letter G as its motif. I picked it carefully up with my handkerchief and took it to the same forensic chap as I had used before. He could find no fingerprint on it and I deposited it in an evidence bag.

I found nothing else of interest on my tour of inspection and decided that it was time to interview the surviving members of the household.

Pamela Menzies had been packed off to bed by her doctor to recover from the shock of seeing her dead husband. But I had no hesitation in invading that sanctum and found her propped up by a plethora of pillows. Throughout the interview, she dabbed at the tears that appeared from time to time in her eyes with a lacy handkerchief that she squeezed into all sorts of shapes with her right hand. She didn't appear initially to be too thrilled to have a man see her without her make up on. But, when she recognised me from my previous visot, she sat up and looked intently at me.

"Anything that I can do to help you find the person who did this terrible thing to my husband, I will willingly do," she said.

"I gather that you occupied separate bedrooms," I began.

"He snored abominably," she replied. "I put up with it for a short time at the beginning of our marriage but then insisted that he slept elsewhere."

"So you didn't hear anything during the course of last night?"

"Not a thing. I am well known to be a very heavy sleeper."

"So who found the body?"

"One of the gardeners," she told me. "When he came on duty, he saw that some of the shrubbery had been broken down and went to investigate. We hadn't realised that George was not in the house. We had assumed that he was having a lie-in and would be late down for breakfast."

"So, have you any idea who would do this to your husband?" I asked.

"Nobody from around here would do such a terrible thing to him, or to anyone else for that matter. It must be connected with the thing that you came to see him about some days ago."

"Did he talk with you about what we discussed on that occasion?"

"He did."

"And did he give you any indication of what it was that actually happened all these years ago while he was in the Army?"

She gave a bit of a sigh.

"We were very open with each other. But he seldom talked about his time during the war. I have found that that is the case with a number of those who served at that time. They don't want to revisit experiences which must often have been horrific."

"But didn't you ask him," I persisted, "whether he and his men had actually come across Nazi loot during the Ardennes Offensive?"

"I did."

"And what did he reply?"

"That it sounded like something out of a Hollywood war movie rather than something that happened in real life. And that they had not had the good luck to have a fortune fall into their laps."

"And did you believe what he had told you?" I quizzed her.

"I did at the time. But I am not so sure now that this horrible thing has happened to him. Perhaps he didn't want to admit, even to me, his wife, that he had done something totally illegal in his youth and then had not benefited from it."

"Does your husband have a pair of cuff links with the letter G on them?" I asked.

She seemed a trifle put out by the sudden change of question and the apparent irrelevance of it but nonetheless answered.

"No, he didn't. His cuff links are silver and do not have letters on them."

"Does anyone in the household or among the

servants smoke cigarettes?"

"My husband's brother does and so does one of the gardeners."

I learned nothing more of interest and went in search of the dead man's younger brother, Geoffrey. He was slimmer than his brother had been, and was less good looking, but he possessed a certain rather devilish charm. He appeared to be very much affected by the death of his brother.

"You came to see George a short time ago, I gather," he said. "Is his death connected with the death of the others that you told him about?"

"It would seem almost certainly so," I replied. "It would be impossible to believe that all the deaths were not connected."

"And it has to do with the time that he spent in the Army? And you believe that it is intimately connected with what he and the others may have stolen and buried while there?"

"It was one suggestion that had been made and that we were following up," I said carefully. "Do you think that it is a likely scenario?"

"It is not something that I would expect of the respectable brother that I have known over the last thirty years or so," he admitted. " I was too young to have been involved in the fighting in the war but I gather that those who did often committed offences that they would never have dreamed of doing during their lives back in civvy street."

"But you have no knowledge of what, if anything, the platoon may have come across in the Ardennes or why they were never able to get their hands on it after the war ended?"

"No idea whatsoever."

"And you heard nothing at all during the course of the night?"

"I take a sleeping pill when I go to bed," he informed me. "I am never in a position to hear anything during the night."

"And you know of no-one who would wish your brother dead?"

"Absolutely not," he said. "He was well liked by everyone in the area. He had no enemies at all, certainly none who were likely to do that terrible kind of torture to him."

I found the son, Peter, in his private office on the ground floor of the house. He was in his early twenties with a round, babyish face, adorned by a small, thin, black moustache that matched his perfectly groomed black hair. He was clad in casual clothes that had cost a pretty penny and he didn't seem to have been all that affected by the death of his father. He was seated at a desk that held the latest type of expensive computer. The desk had a very fancy, very modern telephone on the right and, on the left, was a notepad on which lay a gold-plated pen. He looked up as I entered the room and frowned at the sight of a stranger but he appeared to accept my presence when I informed him who I was.

"You are the person who was here a few days ago to warn him that he was in some possible danger," he said. "It's a pity that he didn't pay more attention to your warning."

"So he told you about it?"

"No, he didn't. He thought that I was too young to be let into the family's darkest secrets. But mother told me all about it. She usually did let me know the things that my father kept from me."

"Had he given her any indication as to what had happened to his platoon during the Ardennes Offensive and whether they had stumbled across Nazi loot or something equally interesting?"

"No, he hadn't," he told me. "But you don't really expect a man to reveal to his wife the unpleasant and possibly illegal things that he had done in his youth. It would tend to destroy whatever illusions that she still retained about him."

"So you believe," I suggested, "that your father and the men under his command did stumble across something valuable while they were on the continent and hung on to it?"

"Why else," he asked, "would someone be knocking them all off after torturing them?"

There was no doubt that he was making a pretty reasonable point.

"Did you hear anything at all during last night?" I asked him.

"Not a thing," he replied. "I slept like a log. Had had quite a bit to drink, you see."

I got the impression that that probably happened most nights.

"It's a tragedy that your mother and your father had decided to occupy separate bedrooms. It was easy for the killer to get at Mr Menzies. It's a great pity that he snored so badly."

Peter gave a somewhat sneering laugh.

"That was at least one of the reasons for separate bedrooms," he said.

I looked at him with interest.

"And what other reasons might there have been?" I enquired.

"Love's young dream doesn't last," he said authoritatively and cynically, sounding rather like an aged philosopher. "People mature in quite different ways and acquire different interests. So that couples inevitably drift apart. And one or other finish up by wishing that they had made a different choice of a lifetime mate."

"And who else held a torch for your mother in her youth?" I asked.

"My uncle lost her to my father. Why do you think that he has never married and lives on here rather than in his own pad?"

I got nothing else of interest from him and it was not long thereafter that I returned to Fettes and reported all that had happened to the Chief Super.

He looked thoughtfully at me when I came to the end of the recital.

"Have you managed to get any idea who is doing all this?" he enquired.

"Edward Mellor is the only surviving member of the platoon," I reminded him, "so he has to be the prime suspect for the killings. But there is always the possibility that one of the platoon told what had happened during the war to a friend and that that friend is now trying to find out where the platoon buried the loot they had found so that he can go back with a metal detecto r and sweep the area to recover it."

"But you have not got the sort of evidence that would convince a jury of who it is that is responsible for all these killings?"

"Unfortunately not."

He heaved a deep sigh.

"When is it that Chief Inspector Forsyth gets back from his holiday?" he asked.

"He is due back on duty tomorrow morning," I informed the Chief Super.

He brightened immediately.

"And you will inform him of all that has happened as soon as he gets in."

"A very detailed report of all that has occurred in his absence will be waiting on his desk for his perusal," I confirmed.

He visibly relaxed and then caught my eye and realised that I would not be best pleased with his obvious relief at the imminent arrival on the scene of the Chief Inspector.

"You and the rest of the team have done a wonderful job in Chief Inspector Forsyth's absence," he said hastily. "Nobody could have done more. But it will be interesting to see if Forsyth can spot something that the rest of us have missed."

"It is kind of you to praise our modest efforts," I replied with my tongue very firmly in my cheek. "But, like you, I will be interested in the Chief Inspector's take on everything that has happened and whether he has any suggestions to make."

I went to the office that I share with three other sergeants and started on the writing of the very detailed report that would be lying ready on the Chief's desk when he put in an appearance on the morrow. It took me a while to get it all down in the necessary detail. I left nothing out. The slightest thing might be of importance. When I had finished, I sat back and thought about what I had just written.

It was while I was doing this that a completely new notion suddenly hit me. I brought it to the front of my mind and examined it carefully for some minutes. I liked it more the more I thought about it. I decided to make a few phone calls to see if I could get any confirmation that my notion had any validity to it. What I heard from the people whom I had rung appeared to confirm that my notion was not just fantasy. I went over everything carefully and felt that I could safely try the notion out that evening on the rest of the squad.

All the facts necessary to deduce who is responsible for the deaths of the former members of the Black Watch platoon are now in your possession. Good luck if you decide to try to work the solution out for yourself before reading the rest of this novel

Alistair MacRae

CHAPTER 8

The rest of the team were already there when I got to the pub that evening. I acquired a pint of heavy at the bar and went and joined them at the table. After a few swallows of the beer, and a few drags on a cigarette, I felt sufficiently revived to go through for them in detail everything that I had experienced that day. They listened attentively and, when I had finished and had another go at the beer, Beaumont made his report.

"We each took one member of the family," he said, "and did a thorough check on them as well as getting information from the locals on the family as a whole. I was looking into the wife."

He paused and imbibed a good draught of beer before continuing.

"Pamela Menzies is well liked around the area, although regarded as a bit on the hoity toity side. She spends her time doing a lot of charitable work and is patron of one or two of the local clubs. The marriage is thought of as stable enough although the pair are not regarded as too starry eyed about one another. There is no-one known as so anti-Menzies that he would wish to do harm to any of the family."

He made it clear that that was all that he had to tell us and picked up his glass. Fletcher put down his pint and took up the story.

"Geoffrey Menzies is regarded as a bit of a wet locally," he explained. "A nice enough fellow but with no go or drive. Just prepared to take what comes to him without making any effort to do better. He had, perhaps still has, a thing about his brother's wife, but is not regarded as likely to do much about it. He is not known to have any consuming interest outside the work that he does on behalf of the estate."

He had a pull at his pint before continuing.

"Like Andy, I didn't find anyone who could think of any reason why anyone would want to kill Menzies. But that's not surprising if the reason for his death is rooted somewhere in the distant past."

Jenkins was, as usual, eager to impress us with how well he had conducted his interviews.

"All the people I spoke to, without exception," he told us, "had no good word to say about Peter Menzies. He appears to be very much a spoiled brat, the result of his parents, particularly his mother, being far too indulgent with him during his youth. There have been a few stories of him trying to act the lord of the manor on some of the local girls when he has had too much to drink, which is all too often. In fact, even his indulgent parents have realised that he is a bit of a menace and have cut down on his allowance and laid down the law and put him on a curfew, thus curtailing his activities in the local area. So he is chafing a bit under the restrictions that have been imposed on him."

He had a swallow of his gin and tonic before continuing.

"But, like Andy and Sid, I could find no one who could think of anybody who would wish Menzies dead."

He sat back in his chair and took a further sip of his gin and tonic.

"I made some enquiries about Mellor," Beaumont informed us. "He was at home all alone with no alibi at the time of the Menzies' killing. And, in addition, it turns out that he is left handed and the size of shoe that he wears is size ten."

"So what?" asked Fletcher. "I thought that we had decided that it wasn't Mellor who was doing all these killings but an acquaintance of one of the members of the troop who wanted to go out there and try to find whatever loot is involved."

"We have to explore all avenues," Beaumont replied. "We can't rule anything out at this stage."

"And it looks as if Mellor is still well in the frame for the killings," suggested Jenkins. "That cuff link that Alistair found hidden out of sight in the Menzies bedroom had the letter G on it and remember that Mellor's Christian name is

Graham."

"If that is the case, shouldn't we be bringing him in here and giving him a really thorough grilling?" asked Fletcher.

I felt that it was time to try out my new theory on the rest of the team.

"I have had a think about the case," I told them, "and I have come up with a new idea about it. Let's see what you think of it."

I took a swig of beer and noted that they were looking at me somewhat sceptically.

"Does it not strike you as a trifle odd," I began, "that the killer has had to torture and kill a number of members of the platoon without apparently learning what it was that he was trying to find out?"

"I don't quite follow what you are trying to get at," admitted Fletcher.

"Why did the person who wanted the detailed information about what had happened during the war while they were in the Ardennes," I enquired, "not ask the person, who had let the incident be known, to give him the information he wanted for a share of the loot if he was able to find it?"

"Maybe the fellow we are looking for wanted all the loot for himself and didn't want to share with anyone," suggested Jenkins.

"So, granted that, why did none of the victims give him the information that he wanted as soon as the torture started? None of them had any hope of finding the loot at this late date and had therefore no reason to withhold the information. Why refuse to give information that was of no use to them and the disclosure of which would stop the most excruciating torture?"

"We thought that, after all this time, memories might be a little dim," Jenkins reminded us.

"Surely at least one of them would remember the details of what must have been one of the most exciting events in his life," I suggested

"It does seem very odd when you put it like that," Beaumont admitted.

"So why didn't they spill the beans right away?" asked Fletcher.

"Maybe the killer wasn't looking for information at all," I offered.

"So what the hell was he wanting from them?" asked Jenkins. "Or are you implying that the killer is a sadistic bastard who gets his kicks from inflicting pain on other people?"

I ignored the question.

"If we are investigating a murder," I asked, "where

would we look initially for the perpetrator?"

"In the family of the victim. Most killings are committed by a member of the immediate family of the victim," said Beaumont.

"So, if you are contemplating the murder of another family member what might you do?"

"Set up another apparent reason for the killing that does not appear to involve you at all," said an enlightened Jenkins.

"So you think that the whole thing about the platoon and getting lost behind enemy lines was just a red herring?" was Fletcher's contribution.

"I don't think that there was ever any loot," I said. "That is what they told us and I think that one of them would have confessed once it was apparent to him that he might be the next victim."

"It makes sense," said Beaumont thoughtfully. "And you think that Menzies was the real victim of all this from the beginning?"

"None of the other members of the platoon, with the possible exception of MacNair, has anything that would be worth going to all this trouble to get your hands on. And why would you keep on with so much future killing if MacNair was the intended victim? And Menzies is, after all, the one with something that another member of the family wants."

"Geoffrey covets his brothers wife," murmured an awed Fletcher.

"And Geoffrey may have cuff links with his initial on them," suggested Jenkins.

"He not only may have, he does own such cuff links," I informed them. "I checked that before I came here. I might also mention that I have checked that Geoffrey is left handed. Furthermore, he smokes cigarettes and it was almost certainly the killer who stamped out the fag end that we found in the Menzies' garden. None of the gardeners or other servants would dare to mar the garden by stamping out a fag end there and then leaving it and a footprint behind. "

Beaumont was looking at me as if seeing me for the first time.

"That's brilliant," he said. "These deductions are worthy of Forsyth."

The others were also looking at me with what appeared to be a new respect, even if mixed with a certain amount of surprise. Jenkins also appeared to be displaying a certain amount of envy.

"Do you think that the wife was in on it as well?" asked Beaumont.

"We will probably never know," I suggested. "Geoffrey

is unlikely to rat on the woman he loves if she was involved."

"Are we going to go and arrest Geoffrey Menzies?" asked Fletcher.

I didn't want to admit that I was not totally confident of my analysis.

"Forsyth is back tomorrow," I pointed out. "He is the boss, after all. I will present him with our solution and leave it to him as to whether we have enough evidence to go to the Procurator Fiscal."

Beaumont clearly felt that the brilliance of my solution deserved better than beer and purchased malt whiskies for three of us and a further gin and tonic for Jenkins. Jenkins and I called a halt after we had consumed that round, leaving the other two to order some food as well as further drinks.

Anna put in an appearance later in the evening and I told her not only of the events of the day but also then revealed my solution to her. She appeared to be mightily impressed though I detected, once again, a hint of surprise mixed in the reaction. I was beginning to wonder more than a little as to what people's idea of my innate intellectual ability really was. But any chagrin at the world's view of my brain's abilities was soon dissipated when she took me to bed and gave me the time of my life as a suitable reward for the cracking of the case. I was a trifle bleary eyed when I staggered in to work the next day. I betook myself to my office and sat there drinking coffee while awaiting the arrival of the great man.

CHAPTER 9

I had got Sergeant Anderson to ring me when Forsyth arrived and I gave the Chief fifteen minutes, enough time for him to read my carefully written report, before I went up and bearded him in his den. He was looking bronzed and fit after his holiday in the sun. He greeted me with a beaming smile.

"I see that you have been kept busy in my absence," he said. "That was a well written report detailing the excellent way in which you have dealt with the latest killings. But I would have expected no less of you. But I also expect that the Chief Superintendent has been giving you a hard time."

"I think," I admitted, "that he was very worried by having to put a mere sergeant in charge of a major murder investigation."

"A sergeant," he said, "who has more ability than most of the inspectors."

"It's very kind of you to say so."

"Have you been able to come to any conclusion as to the identity of the person responsible for all these murders?" he enquired.

"As it happens, I have," I informed him. "The squad discussed the matter last night and came up with a solution to the mystery. Would you be prepared to listen to our analysis?"

"I can think of nothing that would be a better way to begin the resumption of my duties here in Fettes," he replied.

He seated himself comfortably in his chair, leaned back, shut his eyes and brought his fingers together in his lap. He sat quite still as I went carefully through the arguments that I had given to the team the night before. He listened attentively to my discourse and, when I had finished, he remained without moving for several minutes before he opened his eyes, straightened up and gave his response.

"I have to hand it to you," he said. "That was an excellent piece of reasoning. Your demolition of the attempt to get us to believe that the reason for the murders was because of what had happened during the war when the platoon got stranded was exactly the argument that I had come up with myself."

I was flattered that I had worked out that we were being conned by exactly the same reasoning that the Chief had come up with. Though I was a trifle chagrined to find that he had arrived at the same solution so quickly. But I could also see that he was not wholly in agreement with the rest of my reasoning.

"But, from your tone," I said, "I am led to deduce that

you do not believe that Geoffrey Menzies is the murderer we are seeking."

"Would a man," he asked, "who is about to go and knock out his brother and then stage a fake torture session in the garden do so wearing a shirt that needed cuff links? I think not. And, even if he did, would he not notice when he got back to his bedroom and took off his shirt that the cuff link was missing and go and make a thorough search for it immediately and retrieve it long before the police arrived on the scene?"

I felt a bit of a fool for not having realised that the finding of the cuff link was just too convenient.

"So the cuff link was another attempt at misdirection by the killer?"

"It was," he admitted, "along with the footprint that had so conveniently stamped out a cigarette end. Would a killer be so stupid as to choose a muddy area to get rid of a dogend?"

"So we were supposed to realise eventually," I said, "that all the stuff about what happened to the platoon in the war was so much nonsense and then fasten the guilt on Geoffrey?"

"I believe that that is the case."

"So it has to be either the wife or the son who is responsible for all these deaths. Which one do you think it was? Each of them would benefit monetarily from Menzies' death."

"According to your very detailed report," he said, "Menzies escaped and ran through the shrubbery before being struck down by his killer. And the blow that killed him was made by a left handed person. The killer must have been in a complete panic to find that his prisoner had escaped and would strike him down as soon as he got to him to stop him from raising the alarm. So the blow would be instinctive and therefore the left-handedness is genuine. According to your report, Pamela wiped the tears from her eyes with a handkerchief held in her right hand. You found that Geoffrey was left handed. Left handedness tends to run in families and it would therefore be no surprise if his nephew were left handed also. And, indeed, you found that his study had the telephone on the right hand side of his desk and the notepad and pen on the left, which is how a left handed person deals with taking, and recording, telephone calls."

"I suppose that he was the more likely anyway," I pointed out. "To torture and kill a number of people cold bloodedly in order to cover up the real reason for the final crime you have to be enormously self-centred, as Peter was."

"He is clearly a young man who thinks that he is the

most important person in the world and should be able to get whatever he wants. You can magine his chagrin when his parents cut his allowance and imposed a curfew on his movements. The only way that he could see out of his dilemma was to get rid of his father when he would inherit the estate and could do as he pleased."

"You have to be very self conceited," I suggested, "to be prepared to sacrifice a number of veterans in order to cover up the real reason for your criimes."

" And you have to be a bit young and naïve," Forsyth added, "to believe that we would fall for the notion that, after all this time, someone would still be looking for something hidden by troops during the Second World War. And that we would expect that someone about to commit a murder would do so while wearing quite distinctive cuff links."

I went to alert the rest of the squad to the fact that our series of murders had been solved but, unfortunately, that my solution had not been the correct one. Therefore, we had not, once again, beaten Forsyth to the punch and won that coveted case of malt whisky. Beaumont and I then went out to Gorebridge and arrested Peter Menzies. He made no statement when we charged him with the murders and stated hat he had nothing to say until he had seen his solicitor.

The team had a drink in the pub that night to celebrate another victory for the Forsyth team and, at the same time, to drown our sorrows that we had not, once again, got to a solution of a case before Forsyth did so. And, later, I received more, and more interesting, consolation from Anna.

I was summoned to the Chief's office the next morning to find him looking somewhat smug.

"You will be delighted to know," he said, "that, when I presented Peter with the case against him, he confessed to all the murders."

"I am a bit surprised," I said, "that he didn't want to fight it out in court. He seemed very unwilling to talk when I arrested him."

"The fact that I led him to believe that I thought that his plan had been brilliant and that he had only been apprehended by the worst stroke of ill luck may have had something to do with it. I think that he believes that he will now have a place in history among the greatest criminal masterminds of all time."

"Whereas he is a poisonous little toad," I suggested. "with an inflated ego whose intricate plan didn't fool you for a second."

He tried to look somewhat modest with the usual lack of success.

"So another success for you to add to your already long and impressive list of intellectual triumphs," I pointed out.

"A triumph for all of us. The Chief Constable and the Chief Super are, as you might expect, very chuffed and wished their congratulations be conveyed to all of the squad."

"I will let the others know."

"And I add my congratulations to you for some very expert thinking. You didn't get the correct name of the killer but you were within a whisker of doing so. You haven't, unfortunately, earned that case of malt whisky that you have sought for so long but I think that you deserve some tangible recognition for your splendid effort at arriving at a solution."

He delved under his desk and came up with a cardboard container that held four bottles of twenty-five year old Glenlivet.

"I know that the solution was yours alone and, if you decide to retain all four bottles, I think that that is as it should be and no-one will ever know that I have given you these."

I shook my head.

"Our attempts at a solution throughout the years have always been team efforts. The major part of previous solutions were not necessarily always due to me. The fact that the idea for the solution on this occasion was mine does not alter the fact that our attempts to solve cases are joint enterprises. I will share the bottles of malt whisky that you have been good enough to give me with the others."

MISSING

CHAPTER 1

I was sitting in the room which I share with three other sergeants writing a report on that particular July afternoon. It was the report of a successfully completed operation in which Detective Chief Inspector Forsyth had played no part. The case had required for its resolution only hard slog and lots of footwork and had contained no element that called for the use of intellect. Consequently, Forsyth had passed it on to the rest of us to deal with, since that sort of problem contains nothing of interest to him. And, to be honest, he is no good at that type of investigation, something that he would hotly deny, since he regards himself as brilliant at everything.

I had just finished the report and was reading it over when the telephone rang and I was summoned to the Chief's office. I couldn't think of any sin that I had committed recently that he would have heard about and was pretty sure that sins from the past were now well hidden and unlikely to re-emerge, so I went up the stairs without trepidation.

I found Forsyth seated at his desk, looking solemn, and he motioned me to take a seat. I sat down and waited for an explanation of the summons.

"We have been handed a new case to deal with," he told me.

"What kind of a case?" I asked.

"A young boy has gone missing."

"We don't deal with missing person cases," I pointed out. "We are a murder squad. We don't have the expertise for finding kids who have wandered off or been nobbled by paedophiles."

This was not, of course, quite true. We had once been involved in what appeared to be a kidnapping in a case that I have chronicled under the title *Pay the Price* but that had turned out to be a fake.

"The mother of this little boy is a great friend of the wife of the Chief Constable."

"And he is well known," I said, "to be as putty in his wife's hands. So we are being put on to a case that is not in out remit and for which we are not equipped because of nepotism on high."

"We are able to cope with any type of case," he said confidently. "And the Chief Constable said that he wanted the best team in the Lothian and Borders Police to look into the matter for him,"

"So naturally we were chosen."

He didn't even realise that I was being facetious. He thought that I was just stating a known fact.

"So I could hardly refuse to take on the case since he was so flattering and so insistent."

"I suppose not. Who is the little perisher who has gone missing?"

"His name is James Armstrong. He is an only child. His father is a consultant orthopaedic surgeon at the Royal Infirmary, with a very lucrative private practice on the side. I know him slightly, since he is a member of the golf club to which I belong, though he is not one of my favourite people. His wife is an advocate, very highly thought of and successful, who is also very active in both charitable and in feminist causes."

"I can see," I said, "that I am going to have an enjoyable time mixing with the cream of the Edinburgh elite. Have we any idea what may have happened to the missing son?"

"None at all. You might alert the rest of the squad to our latest assignment. You should allocate to them the tasks of doing some background checks on the family, their servants and their friends. I will meet you in the car park in five minutes."

I was leaning against the car, enjoying the sun, when he put in an appearance. I got into the driver's seat and watched with the usual interest as he rolled his large bulk into a ball and shot it sideways into the car. I put up a restraining hand to keep him from crushing me against the door and waited until he had belted up before starting off.

Forsyth hates to be driven only slightly less than he hates driving himself. Like all great men, he is a bit neurotic. He is convinced that most of the rest of the populace, once ensconced in a car, become homicidal, not only intent on finishing off their own lives in a monumental accident, but in taking with them as many of the rest of humanity, Forsyth not excluded, as they can. This fantasy, not without some foundation in our car ridden city, is a product of his being entirely at the mercy of others in a car, something that he would not tolerate in any other sphere of his life. The result of all this paranoia is that I tend to drive, when I have him alone and defenceless in the car with me, a little faster than I normally would, and a lot faster than he would consider to be safe, to get a little of my own back on him for his making us do all his routine and uninteresting work for him.

That day was par for the course. He looked anxious as we drove from the Headquarters building in Fettes through the town centre to the south side of the city but made no comment about my driving or any suggestion that I slowed down. But I think that he was relieved when we arrived safely at the Armstrong residence which was a two storey stone building in fair sized grounds, sheltered from the vulgar gaze by the high wall that surrounded the property.

The entrance to the property was by gates that were a masterpiece of the ironmaker's craft. I had to get out of the car to open these since no-one was stationed there to do the task nor was there anyone within sight of us who could be press-ganged into doing it. The gates were nicely balanced and opened easily. I carefully shut them behind us and drove in and parked in front of the house. A woman of about thirty had emerged from the building. From her uniform-like dress, I assumed that she was a servant. She asked us if we were the expected police officers and, when we replied in the affirmative, she escorted us into the house.

As we moved through the sumptuous entrance hall to the sitting room, I was impressed by the good taste of the people who had furnished it. But whether this had been done by the owners or by professional designers I was never able to find out. In the sitting room, we found Mrs Hillary Armstrong ensconced in a comfortable and well designed armchair. She rose to greet us. She was a tall, willowy woman, quite good looking but with a rather hard cast to her features. And there was a certain steeliness in her cold blue eyes that made me imagine that she would be a formidable opponent not only in a court of law but also in everyday life. She was wearing trousers and a cashmere sweater.

"I recognise you, Mr Forsyth," she greeted the Chief, "from functions at the golf club."

"And I have seen you working your magic in court," he replied gallantly, not to be outdone. "This is Sergeant MacRae. It is tragic that we should meet once again under these circumstances. We would like some details of how your son was found to be missing. For a start, how old is James?"

"He is four years old. My husband and I are very busy professional people," she pointed out, "so we naturally employ a nanny to look after James's needs. She lives here in the house with us and we treat her as one of the family. She is accustomed to let him play in the garden when the weather is fine as it has been today."

"And it was from the garden that James was taken?" I asked.

"It was. There is an area at the rear of the house that has been fenced off. It contains a swing, a slide and other pieces of apparatus with which children like to play. Jennifer left him there while she went into the house to prepare his lunch. It is perfectly safe there. She has never had any worry about leaving him there alone, nor have we. When she returned, she found that he was gone. She looked everywhere but it was obvious that he could not have vanished on his own. She called me. I came as soon as I could. My husband is in the middle of a rather delicate operation and cannot be disturbed. But he has been informed of the situation and will be here as quickly as he can."

"So you believe that someone has abducted your son?" asked Forsyth.

"It seems that there can be no other explanation of his disappearance."

"But you have received no demand for a ransom to get him back?"

"None has so far come," she informed us. "But I am sure that one will come in due course. The alternative explanation of his disappearance is too horrible to contemplate."

I suppose that it is better to hope that money will bring your son back rather than that he is in the grasp of a paedophile or of someone seeking revenge for a perceived wrong.

"And you have not seen any unfamiliar persons hanging around the area recently or heard of anyone who has been doing so?" I asked.

"It is a very select area," she pointed out. "Anyone hanging around would be very noticeable and would be asked to leave. And, if they did not do so, the police would be called."

"We will need a photograph of your son, if that is possible," I said.

She crossed over to a side table and took from it a photograph in an ornate frame and handed to to me. It was a studio portrait showing a young boy standing by a rocking horse looking into the camera. He had a shock of blonde hair above a round face that held a somewhat guarded expression. There was a hint of sadness in the soulful brown eyes.

"That will do very nicely," I assured her.

"I think," said Forsyth, "that we had better have a word with the lady whom you employ as a nanny. I assume that she was the person who greeted us and showed us in. What is her name?"

"Her name is Jennifer Clarkson. I may say that she comes from a good family. Her mother was in service with my father."

Mrs Armstrong departed on her errand and shortly thereafter the woman who had shown us in came into the room and stood demurely in front of us. Forsyth suggested that she sat down and she did so rather gingerly on one of the upright chairs.

I studied her a bit more closely this time round. She was quite a pretty thing in a rather washed out way. She was of medium height and on the thin side with straight black hair cut short. She didn't seem all that overawed by being grilled by two important policemen.

We took her through what had happened that morning. Her account was exactly the same as that of her mistress. She had left James alone in the play area in order that she could get his lunch prepared. This was quite her usual practice. But, when she had returned on this occasion, the boy was no longer there and there was no way in which he could have got out of the fenced-off area on his own. She had searched everywhere that he might have been had he somehow managed to get out of the play area. But he was not anywhere within the outer wall. And she had been forced to assume that he had been kidnapped. She had alerted Mrs Armstrong to what had occurred and it was the latter who, when she arrived, had called the police.

"Who would know," I asked, "that James would be playing in the area at the back of the house on a good day like this?"

"Any friend of the family," she suggested, "would know that that was likely, as would all of my friends and most of the tradesmen who call here regularly. But anyone who has ever been here for whatever reason, and has seen the play area, would be likely to guess that he would be playing here on a good day."

"And you haven't seen any strangers hanging around the place recently?"

"No, I haven't," she said. "Strangers hanging around here would stand out like a sore thumb and would be asked to move on."

"And no-one has attempted to talk to you in a pub or restaurant lately?"

"I am seldom in pubs or restaurants. And no-one has engaged me in conversation there or anywhere else recently."

"Do the Armstrongs employ a gardener?" Forsyth enquired.

"They do."

"And where was he at the time that the boy went missing?"

"He had gone off on his lunch break."

"How very convenient," I observed. "The whole thing was very well timed."

"I gather that your mother served Mrs Armstrong's father," said the Chief. "Is this how how obtained your current position?"

"Mrs Armstrong's father owns a large estate on the west side of Edinburgh. Many of the people who live round about there work for her father in one capacity or another. Once James was born, it was obvious that Mrs Armstrong would be looking for a nanny for the boy and her father made sure that the position went to someone whom he knew all about and whom he believed would be capable of doing a good job."

There was a bit of a commotion out in the entrance hall and then a man burst into the sitting room. He was a tall, handsome man in his late thirties with straight brown hair, fashionably cut, who was dressed in an expensive suit with matching tie. There was a hint of worry in his cold blue eyes and around his mouth. I assumed that he was the surgeon father who was wealthy enough to be a member of Forsyth's very exclusive golf club, and this was proved to be correct when his eye fell on the Chief and he recognised him.

"Ah, Forsyth," he said. "I heard that you had been called in. Have you any news of James?"

"We have only just arrived," the Chief replied, "and are in process of determining the facts. It is too early for there to be any progress."

"Have you any idea of what could have happened to James?"

"It seems most likely that he has been kidnapped for ransom," suggested the Chief, not wanting to bring up the more horrific alternatives. "You are a wealthy family. To steal James would seem to a criminal a good source of easy money."

"But, when the Lindberg baby was kidnapped, he was killed even after the ransom had been paid," Armstrong pointed out.

"That is the exception. Most kidnapped children are returned safely to their families after the ransom has been paid."

Mrs Armstrong came in, no doubt having heard the commotion caused by her husband's entry. They greeted each other rather formally.

"We would like to station an officer in the house," I said before they could get carried away, "one who would listen in to any phone calls that come through and who would also put a recording machine on to your phone so that any ransom demand made would be on record and could be studied for clues."

"Of course," Armstrong replied at once. "Anything to help you bring back James and bring to justice the people responsible for this terrible act."

We left them to discuss the situation among themselves while we went and had a look around the play area. Not far from it, we found that there were two marks in the grass next to the wall where a ladder had recently stood and where enough weight had been placed on it to leave the marks. On the corresponding area outside the wall we found a set of similar marks. Not far away we discovered that a ladder had been pushed into some bushes. It was an expanding one that could be bought in many a hardware store. When the ladder was later tested, it held no fingerprints.

"It looks as if the kidnapper was waiting for the nanny to go off," I said, "and then climbed onto the wall, brought the ladder over, chloroformed the kid and then carried him to a waiting car."

"It does look that way," Forsyth agreed.

The area between the wall and a nearby large wood was occupied by a minor road and a number of fields in which grew barley and potatoes. There was no habitation in sight.

"Not much chance of being overlooked while you snatched the kid," I pointed out.

"Just the place to operate from if you are intending to perform a kidnapping," Forsyth agreed.

We had a word with the gardener, Alex Beatty. He proved to be a youngish man with a marked local accent, a round, weather-beaten face and luxuriant blond hair.

"I was having a sandwich in the greenhouse when the lad was taken," he said in answer to my first question. "It was my lunch break."

"And you heard and saw nothing?" I asked.

"Not a thing."

"Would you have heard if the boy had cried out?"

"Probably. But he was a very quiet and trusting little boy. He would almost certainly have gone along willingly if the kidnapper had spoken kindly to him and offered him a sweet."

"And when did you hear about what had happened to James?"

"When Miss Clarkson came to find me. She told me that the boy was missing and said that she had looked everywhere. I had a look round as well but he was nowhere to be seen."

"And what do you think has happened to him?" I enquired.

He looked a trifle askance at me.

"Well, he's been kidnapped, hasn't he? The Armstrongs have lots of money. They'll get the lad back if they pay up."

"And have you seen any odd strangers around here lately?" I quizzed.

"There's been no-one around the place that I've noticed."

The copper who was going to man the telephone and fit up the recorder arrived and we introduced him to the Armstrongs. After the exchange of a few more remarks, we left and made our way back to Fettes. Forsyth went up to his office, no doubt to brood on what we had learned, and, since it was now past five o'clock, I wended my way to the hostelry where we relax after a hard day's work. It lies halfway between the Police Headquarters at Fettes and the Crematorium. We always occupy the same table, one that is far enough away from the bar counter and any other table so that there is no danger that our words of wisdom might fall on flapping ears and appear in garbled form in the next day's *Scotsman*. None of the rest of the team were there, so I acquired a pint of heavy and went to our table where I lit a cigarette and had a long swallow of the amber liquid. The other three gradually appeared, also got pints and then joined me. I handed round cigarettes and allowed them to slake their thirsts before starting the evening proceedings.

As you are aware, the Forsyth team always meets in the pub to try to arrive at the solution of whatever mystery we are involved in before the great man does. All right, so this was not a normal murder case where we would be looking to solve the problem and beat Forsyth to the punch. But ingrained habits are hard to overcome and we operated on this occasion as on any other.

I started by telling them everything that Forsyth and I had come across that day. Some squads tend to keep the lower echelons in the dark. They see no reason why the rank and file should know what is going on. But I believe in letting every member of a squad know all that has been discovered. The rawest recruit is as capable of coming up with the bright idea that solves a case as is a grizzled veteran. But he cannot do that unless he is aware of all that has been discovered. When I had finished, I had a long draught of beer and then suggested that Andy Beaumont should now enlighten us on whatever it was that he had discovered.

"I have been talking to the people who live in the area around the Armstrong place," he told us, "getting a feel for what they are like and how they are regarded. Armstrong is one of the top surgeons in this neck of the woods and charges top fees. He is dedicated to his work and intent on making as much money as he can while he is able to. In consequence, he doesn't spend all that amount of time with the wife and family, certainly not as much as he should. A nice enough bloke, apparently, but driven by ambition and somewhat self-centred."

He had a pull at his pint before continuing.

"I had a look at whether there was anyone in his background who might have such a grudge against him that it was big enough to make him want to take it out on the son."

"And there is such a one?" I asked.

"A fellow called Benson. Armstrong did an operation on him that didn't go well. The surgeon and the lawyers for the hospital claimed that this happened because Benson had not disclosed an underlying condition to them. Had they been told, they would never have attempted to perform the operation. And they were vindicated in a law suit. But Benson blames Armstrong for his present unhappy condition and has sworn to get revenge one way or another."

"We will certainly look at him very carefully," I promised.

"And I find that Mrs Armstrong was of much the same type as her husband," Beaumont went on. "Perhaps that is what drew them together. She comes from a wealthy family anyway but seems intent on becoming the lawyer whom every client wants. She has made a name for herself by successfully defending a number of important clients in high profile cases and looks to be going from strength to strength. But this means that both of them lead very busy lives and neither parent spends a lot of time with young James. So what affection he gets is provided by the nanny who appears to be very competent and well regarded by all."

"And has the competent Mrs Armstrong got any

enemies who might wish to get at her through the boy?" I queried.

"As a matter of fact there is. A man called Charters was done out of most of his money by a fraudulent scheme. Charters took the fraudster to court but Mrs Armstrong, as defence counsel, used a legal technicality to get her client off the hook. As a result, Charters' wife committed suicide when she found that they were penniless and would have to sell their long time home. Charters has vowed to get his own back on Mrs Armstrong whom he blames for his wife's death."

"Charters is another whom we will have to look into," I observed.

Beaumont made it clear that he was finished and Sid Fletcher took up the story.

"Kidnappers often have someone on the inside who is providing them with the necessary information, So I was going into the background and contacts of the nanny, Jennifer Clarkson. She comes from a family who have worked for Mrs Armstrong's parents for many years. She is a quiet girl who doesn't have a flamboyant life outside her job and doesn't have expensive outside interests. And there is no record of her being seen talking to strangers around the place or on her days off."

He paused and had a swallow from his pint before

continuing.

"I also looked into the gardener He is not known to have had any contact with outsiders recently. But he does have convictions for petty theft when he was a teenager and is said to have ambitions to hit the big time, though this is unlikely to happen as long as he remains a gardener. Furthermore it is said that the nanny is badly smitten by him."

"So you are suggesting," I said, "that he might have persuaded the Clarkson woman to join him, and possibly others, in staging the kidnapping of James to give them the necessary cash to allow them to lead a high powered life elsewhere?"

"It looks like a good possibility," he maintained. "It would be very easy for the two of them together to arrange the kidnapping of the boy with no-one else around for most of the time in that isolated house."

"It would indeed," I agreed.

I turned to Marion Telford and asked how she had got on. She is the latest addition to Forsyth's team. Some years ago, the powers that be realised that not enough women were getting into the detective squads and decided that, as vacancies occurred, members of the fair sex should be introduced into the existing teams. When it came to our turn, I have to admit that I had had grave doubts about having a woman in the squad, not because I have anything against female employees (some of my best friends are women!), but because I was doubtful about how Forsyth would view having a female DC working for him.

The great man was at one time married but the union, as I said earlier, ended in a very acrimonious divorce. This may explain why he is now so concerned never to be found to be in the wrong and why he always plays his cards so close to his chest. I'm not privy to the secrets of the great man's private life so I have no idea what part sex plays in it. But, for reasons that I have never understood, Forsyth goes down big with women. I suppose that he's quite good looking and maybe females sense the presence of that massive intellect and that turns them on. He's a bit nauseating in female company because he feels he has to put on a bit of a show for them. Or maybe I'm overreacting because I'm just a tad jealous. Who knows? But I was afraid that he might feel that he couldn't be his natural self when involved in tricky cases in the presence of a woman. But, to my surprise, he'd accepted the first one without a murmur and had, since then, treated our female members no differently than the rest of the squad.

The first woman on the squad, Sandra Cockburn, had been a rampant feminist, but had fitted in well and not given Andy and Sid any reason not to be happy with the new set up. The second, Penny Patterson, had been the most beautiful woman that I had ever known and in time I had had an affair with her, perhaps the most rewarding that I will ever have. It was a sad day when she received promotion as a sergeant in a newly formed unit that was to look into organised crime in Scotland. Marion Telford was her replacement.

In contrast to Penny, Marion was on the plain side. I gathered that that had led to her being bullied at school. But, being the determined person she is, she had learned judo and put a stop to the bullying by giving the bullies a taste of their own medicine by effortlessly throwing them around the playground. She had added further martial arts to her repertoire and that had proved handy during her time as a copper on the beat.

She had arrived on our squad somewhat in awe of Forsyth because of his reputation, but had become somewhat disillusioned by his piling all the tedious routine work on his subordinates. But then he had solved a case that had had the rest of us totally at sea by some brilliant deductions and, like many a DC before her, she had come down with a terrible case of hero worship. But we had worked on her, giving her all the most uninspiring and tedious jobs that Forsyth piled on us and had, by the time that the Armstrong kidnapping hit us, got her back to near normality.

"I talked to the people who live or work in the area of the Armstrong residence," Marion told us. "There aren't all that many of them and only one had seen anything of interest. No strangers have been seen having a look round the place and the only one who saw anything on the day that James was kidnapped was the farmer who owns the fields at the back of the house. He drove down the road that skirts the property in a tractor at about lunch time and says that there was a car parked on the road near to the house. He didn't think anything of it at the time because the wood contains some interesting flora and fauna and people often park a car on the road and follow a track that runs to the wood."

"And, of course, he didn't bother to make a note of the car number so that we would be able to trace it," suggested Beaumont.

"There was no reason for him to do that," Marion pointed out. "The car was an expensive one. He thinks that it was a Mercedes but he wouldn't swear to it in a court of law."

"And he didn't see anyone around or in the car, I suppose," said Fletcher.

"No. But a tractor is noisy and anyone around would duck down when they heard it coming and would stay out of sight until the farmer was past."

"So, although we have possible suspects, we have no leads to the kidnapper," I said thoughtfully. "We can only hope that a ransom demand comes in and we can get a pointer to who is responsible when they pick the money up."

"So you think that it is a kidnapper, rather than a paedophile, who has done the snatching of James?" asked Marion.

"It seems the more likely. And it would present a better possible outcome for the kid."

We had another round of pints and discussed other things before we broke up. I reported all that the team had found out to Forsyth the next morning and he admitted that there was nothing to go on until a ransom demand or further evidence surfaced.

CHAPTER 3

It was later on that same afternoon that we were informed that a ransom demand had been phoned through to the Armstrong household. We drove down to the house where we found both of the Armstrongs and a Barry Mercer discussing the next move. The latter was a smartly dressed man of about the same age as the Armstrongs, well built, rather like a prop forward, with blond, wavy hair and a cheerful face in which were bright brown eyes which, at that moment, held a look of concern. It turned out that he was another doctor who had been at University with the Armstrongs. He had gone into medical research with a research establishment and had made quite a name for himself in that line. He had stayed as Armstrong's best friend and was also godfather to young James. He had joined them to render whatever assistance, financial or otherwise, that might be required.

We listened to the recording of the phone call that had been received. A male voice that had been put through some distorting device, and which spoke with a marked, but obviously put on, broad Scottish accent, declared that he had James and that the boy would be released unharmed once a quarter of a million pounds in used, non-sequential notes of low denomination had been paid. Instructions for the delivery of the money would be issued in five days time to give the Armstrongs the necessary time to get the money together. And they should make sure that the police did not attempt to interfere in any way with the payment of the ransom.

"Did they trace where the call was made from?" I asked the copper who had been guarding the phone, waiting for the call.

"There wasn't enough time for them to trace the call before he had rung off," he replied. "But the call was made from an isolated call box on the southern outskirts of the city. There was, of course, no-one there when the nearest patrol car got to it. And there had been no-one around to see who it was who had made the call."

Forsyth had, in the meantime, got the attention of the Armstrongs.

"Can you raise the quarter of a million demanded?" asked the Chief.

"We had already spoken to various people who could help us raise the money, and to the bank," Armstrong told him. "There should be no difficulty in having the cash ready for when the bastard calls again."

"We will provide the container in which you will place the money to be transported to the drop off point," Forsyth informed them. "It will have a built-in tracking device and there will be another similar device which we will insert into the middle of the notes."

"Won't the kidnappers regard that as the police interfering with the delivery of the money?" said Mrs Armstrong nervously.

"Kidnappers issue these sorts of instructions and threats to try to scare you into shutting the police out. But you should not allow them to intimidate you. They will almost certainly," Forsyth added soothingly, "release James once they have the cash. But, just in case they don't, it is as well to have a method of tracing their whereabouts. And I am sure that, once you have James back safely, you would wish us to be able to arrest the kidnappers and recover the money."

She and the other two agreed that trackers were desirable and, after a little further discussion, we left them to the task of collecting the cash and promised to return to the house with the necessary equipment in a further five days' time.

Nothing else connected with the kidnapping surfaced during those five days, and it was early on the fifth day that we presented ourselves again at the Armstrong residence. Mercer arrived shortly after us. We had brought the bag with the tracker incorporated and we loaded into it the money, slipping into one of the bundles of notes the other tracking device. Thereafter we sat around, drinking coffee, awaiting the expected phone call. When it came, we all huddled round the phone expectantly. The officer switched to loudspeaker and announced the number. An immediate message came through.

"Mr Armstrong will put the money in a bag," said the same broad Scottish, distorted voice, "and drive with it in his car, without any walkie talkie or other communication device, to the telephone box at the corner of Harrison Road and Harrison Gardens. A message will come through to that box at precisely ten o'clock containing instructions as to where to leave the money. No-one must follow the car or the boy will not be released."

The voice cut off as soon as the message was finished. The cop switched off the phone.

"You see the need for the tracking device," I said. "Mr Armstrong will be completely out of touch once he leaves here and we will have no idea where he will be told to deliver the money."

"Where the hell is Harrison Road located?" asked Armstrong.

"It is on the West side of the city," I told him. "It's south of Gorgie and off the Slateford Road."

"You will find it easily enough," said Mercer. "We will show you where it is on the map. And you have plenty of time to get there."

"Write the destination you are given by the next phone call on a pad," said Forsyth, "and leave it for us in the phone box. It gives us another chance of staying in touch with you."

The phone rang. The officer in charge answered it, listened to what was said for a few seconds and then turned to us.

"That call was made from a phone box in Slateford. There was no-one there when a patrol car got to it and there was no-one around who could give them a description of the person who had been making use of the phone."

I had given a phone call to Marion as soon as the instructions for the payment had come through and she was able to get to Harrison Park, which was bordered on two of its sides by Harrison Road and Harrison Gardens, before Armstrong reached the area. She left her car on the opposite side of the park from the phone box and was strolling casually along the edge of the park when Armstrong arrived and entered the booth. She heard the phone ring, saw him take the call and then leave. There seemed to be no-one else in the area. Nonetheless, she went unhurriedly to the box, looked at the pad that Armstrong had left, which named a further phone box in the Balgreen area to which he had to go to. She then phoned me and gave me the information.

It turned out that, when Armstrong got the next message at the phone box in Balgreen, he was told to return to Harrison Park and to then leave the bag containing the ransom money in a particular litter bin on the opposite side of the park from the phone box. Armstrong did as he had been instructed and then drove home to await developments.

Two cars had been keeping in touch with the tracking device, following a similar route to the one taken by Armstrong but on parallel streets so that anyone keeping tabs on Armstrong would not observe the following vehicles. When Armstong's car moved on but the tracker remained stationary, the following cars knew that a pick-up was likely to be imminent and got ready. The occupants of one of the cars, a young couple, left their car and strolled hand in hand into the park, seated themselves on a bench, from which they had a view of the litter bin and appeared to be indulging in a spot of necking.

It was not long before a young man, very casually dressed, entered the park and made a bee line for the litter bin. He paid no attention to the necking couple and lifted the bag from the bin and headed out of the park. When he was out of sight, the couple got up, ran back to their car and joined the other as they kept track of the man and the bag.

It was a short time later that the phone rang at the Armstrong house and we were informed that the man who had collected the bag had finished up in a house in the Shandon Colonies. There seemed to be no-one but the man in the house and, so far, no-one had gone in or come out and no-one appeared to be keeping an eye on that particular residence. We drove to the area and liaised with the officers there, but kept well out of sight of the target house.

We were told that the officers already there had determined that the house was owned by a certain Walter Stalker, who had a string of convictions over the last few years for minor crimes including breach of the peace when under the influence of drink or drugs. We waited for a time to see whether anyone would approach the house but when, after a fair amount of time, no-one did, Forsyth made the decision to storm the house. The front door was broken down and the house was invaded, armed officers leading the way. Stalker, who offered no resistance and seemed totally bemused by what was happening to him, was grabbed and handcuffed. The house was searched thoroughly but there was no James, or indeed anyone else, on the premises.

We returned to the living room and confronted Stalker

who was now sitting in a chair guarded by two of the armed officers.

"Where have you put James Armstrong?" asked Forsyth.

"Who?"

Stalker seemed to be genuinely puzzled by the question.

"The kidnapped boy whose ransom you have just collected from Harrison Park."

"Kidnap? Ransom? What the hell are you talking about?"

"You have recently collected a bag from a refuse bin in Harrison Park. That bag contained bank notes to the value of a quarter of a million pounds, which was the ransom paid by his parents to secure the release of James Armstrong," I pointed out.

"A quarter of a million pounds," he mouthed. "You're kidding?"

"You didn't look in the bag?"

"I have enough sense,"he said, "not to meddle in things that could get you a broken leg or even a broken neck."

"So what did you think was in the bag that you collected?" enquired Forsyth.

Stalker was only too eager to tell us his side of the

story.

"I was in the pub on my own, wasn't I, having a drink a couple of nights ago and this fellow sits down beside me and offers me two hundred quid to do a job for him, one hundred there and then and another hundred once the job was done."

"And the job was to pick up a bag from Harrison Park today?" I suggested.

"Right on."

"And why wasn't he able to pick the bag up himself and save himself having to pay out a couple of hundred quid?"

"Well, it was dodgy, wasn't it? You don't shell out a couple of hundred for nothing, do you? He didn't want whoever it was paying up finding out who was getting the cash."

"You did not mind the payer thinking it was you who was getting the money?" asked the Chief.

"If he put a watch on the money, he would realise that I wasn't the one screwing him, that I was only the messenger. And you have to take a wee bit of a risk for that amount of money. I didn't expect that the polis would be involved."

"So what was the man who asked you to do this like?" I asked.

"He was just a man."

"You'll have to do better than that. Was he tall or short?"

"Medium, I think. But he was sitting down at the table, so it was difficult to judge. And he was wearing a battered old hat that he had pulled well down over his face and he had on dark glasses, so you couldn't see all that much of him."

"How old was he?"

"Older than me by quite a bit but by how much it was difficult to tell."

"What clothes was he wearing?"

"An old, dark raincoat over what looked like dark flannel trousers."

"All of which, as well as the hat, have since been dumped in a bin somewhere well away from where chummy lives," I observed.

"Have you ever seen the man before?" Forsyth enquired.

"Not that I can ever remember."

"And is there nothing at all that you can remember about him that was distinctive?"

Stalker thought about it for a while.

"Well, he did speak with a lisp."

And that was as much as we could get out of him.

Both Forsyth and I believed that Stalker was telling us the truth about why he had picked up the bag. Kidnapping was not in his line at all. It was way out of his league. And it made sense that the kidnappers would put a loser, someone just like Stalker, in our path in case we had followed the money. That way they could find out whether it was safe to collect the ransom.

We took Stalker down to Police Headquarters and charged him before driving to the Armstrong residence to return the ransom to its rightful owners. When we got there, we found that three very angry people were awaiting our arrival.

"We should never have allowed you to be involved in this thing at all," Mrs Armstrong said venomously. "I might have known that representatives of the police were not likely to have the brains to make sure that they didn't foul the whole thing up."

I didn't feel like reminding her that she had asked for us in the first place.

"While you were out messing things up, the kidnappers have made a call to us," she went on, "saying that, because we have not followed their instructions to the letter, but have called in the police, we will never set eyes on James again."

"They will not give up their hope of getting the ransom

that easily," said Forsyth confidently. "They are attempting to terrify you, so that, when they come up with the next demand, you will keep us out of the payment process and they will be able to collect the money without fear of being detected."

"I hope for your sake that you are right," said Armstrong. "And you can take it from me that you will receive no information from us as to any further demands from the kidnappers. The officer recording the phone calls has already been sent away. And now I would be grateful if you would leave my house."

I think that, in his state of almost uncontrollable anger, he had to stop himself from adding 'and never darken my door again'.

We departed from the house with our tails very definitely between our legs. When we were outside, I turned to Forsyth.

"Are you going to let the Armstrongs pay the next ransom demand without any interference at all from us?" I enquired.

"We will tap their telephone at the exchange," he replied, "so that we are kept informed of what is going on. But I think that we will have to let them pay the ransom without overt interference from us."

"Does that mean that there will be covert

interference?"

"I think," he said, "that we should keep a discreet watch on what is taking place. We must not be the cause of the payment process being aborted for a second time. But I would like to have a reasonable chance of bringing these kidnappers to justice should anything go wrong the next time round."

"You are confident that the kidnappers will make a second attempt to get their money?"

"Of course. If you have spent a good deal of time and effort on such a scheme, you are not going to pack it all in after the first setback. And they will be confident that the Armstrong will be so scared of what could happen if things go wrong again, that they will keep us out of the loop the next time round."

CHAPTER 3

After five days, no further demand for ransom had gone to the house over the telephone, as we knew since the Armstrong phone had been tapped at the exchange. I made discreet enquiries which revealed that the Armstrongs were becoming more restive and alarmed every day that passed. This suggested that no message by other means had been received by them. I was beginning to get a trifle worried, so I went upstairs and tapped on the door of Forsyth's office. He told me to come in, greeted me courteously, offered me a seat and enquired what he could do for me.

"I am getting worried," I told him. "If we were right in believing that the last message from the kidnappers was intended to scare the Armstrongs shitless and make sure that they would keep us out of the loop the next time round, wouldn't professionals have struck while the iron was hot and have been in touch again with the Armstrongs by this time?"

He heaved a sigh.

"I have had the same worry," he assured me. "I can see no reason why the kidnappers would delay a further message this long."

I decided that I had to bring up the unmentionable thing.

"Do you think that we have perhaps got it totally wrong?"

It was difficult for him to admit, even to me, that he had got anything wrong. But, after a moment of silence, he said it.

"I am coming to the conclusion that we might not have got it right."

"So, if the kidnappers are giving up after the first failed attempt, does this mean either that the kidnappers are amateurs like Beatty and Clarkson who have been scared by what has happened or that the kidnapping was never about money at all?"

"It rather looks that way."

"So the demand for a large ransom to be paid," I suggested, "may just have been an attempt to throw suspicion away from the real purpose of the kidnapping of the boy."

"That could well be the case."

I thought about it.

"We abandoned looking into the other possible reasons for the kidnapping that we had suggested," I pointed out, "once the ransom demand came in. It looks as if it would be a good idea to get the team to dig into the movements of the names that we had come up with as possibles initially."

"That would certainly be worth doing," he agreed. "Remind me of the names the squad had come across."

I dug into my memory.

"We thought that the nanny, Clarkson and the gardener, Beatty, might be in cahoots," I began. "And I suppose that it's possible that they might have been scared off by us picking up Stalker and be afraid to have a second go."

"It is a possibility," he said.

"There is also a George Benson," I went on, "who believes that his present precarious hold on life is due to Armstong making a mess of an operation he performed on him. And we came across a Melville Charters who hates Mrs Armstrong's guts because she used a legal nicety to prevent him from getting compensation for a fraud perpetrated on him and because his wife committed suicide as a result."

"Then we should get as much information about these people and what they have been doing since the kidnapping as we can."

"And I would like to do a blanket job on Barry Mercer as well?"

"Why Mr Mercer?"

"Why has he been poking his nose in ever since the kidnapping took place?"

"He has been a good friend of both of them since his university days," he pointed out, "and he is the boy's godfather."

"I think that he was in love with Mrs Armstrong in their early days. Maybe still is. It is just possible that he hates her for spurning him and him for sneaking away the woman he loved. It was very convenient for him to be around and know everything that was going on if he was involved in the kidnapping."

"It will do no harm to include Mercer in the survey," he indicated, "even although your notion seems a trifle far-fetched."

So I went back down and got a hold of the other three members of the squad. I told Beaumont to find out everything that he could about Clarkson and Beatty, Fletcher to do a similar job on Benson, and Telford to look thoroughly into Charters. I would spend my time looking into the background of Mercer. We would all meet in the pub to report progress later on that evening.

By the time I got back to Fettes that evening I was feeling more than a little fatigued. The prospect of a drink was very inviting and I hastened to our watering hole. I found that Sid and Marion were already there and Andy was not long behind me. When we had all revived our spirits and our strength with the aid of the alcohol and had

had a sufficient intake of nicotine, I let them know how I had fared with my enquiries.

"Mercer is apparently looked on by almost everyone," I told them, "as one of the good guys. And, even his few detractors wouldn't see him as someone who would kill a young lad. He lives very comfortably, looked after by a valet who had worked for his father until his death. Mercer did well at university, which is why he now has a top job in a research establishment. And, while a student, he had a genuinely deep friendship with both Armstrong and the lady who became Mrs Armstrong. It seems that he was in love with the lady but, on the surface at least, harbours no feelings of resentment to Armstrong for his taking the lady away from him. And he seems to take his job of godfather very seriously, spending a lot of time trying to make sure that the kid is brought up in the right way and has what he needs. And I gather that the kid dotes on him. He probably gets more attention from him than he gets from his parents."

I paused to have a drink of beer.

"I have to admit that my notion that Mercer might be harbouring feelings of hatred towards both the Armstrongs and might have sought to revenge himself on them by harming the kid seems to be well wide of the mark. It is just not on"

Beaumont put down his pint, after taking a deep draught of the liquid, and took his turn at the reporting of progress.

"Beatty strikes me as the type of man who will always be looking for an easy way to make lots of money," he said. "I imagine that's why he has a record. And he is just the sort to think that snatching a kid could net him a fortune. And Clarkson seems to be so besotted with him that she would go along with whatever he suggested that they do. The Armstrongs are normally very busy furthering their own careers, so that both the servants are given a pretty free hand as to what they do. So there is little supervision as to where they are at any time anyway. And, during the time that the kid was missing, the Armstrongs had more pressing concerns than bothering about where the nanny and the gardener were at any time. And the house is fairly isolated so there is no-one around to see who is going out and coming in so they could both have made phone calls or hired Stalker to pick up the cash without anyone being the wiser."

He stopped and had a swallow of beer.

"But, if it was they who took the boy," asked Fletcher, "why hasn't there been another demand from them for the ransom?"

"They were probably quite scared," Beaumont

suggested, "by the fact that Stalker was picked up so quickly by us. But I can't see them either being prepared to kill the kid or to give up now and lose the chance of getting a fortune. So I reckon that they are biding their time before making another move, either in the hope that police surveillance will be discontinued or while they work out a fail-safe way of getting the money without being nabbed in the process."

"So what is your considered opinion?" I asked. "Would you believe that the pair are the ones behind the kidnapping?"

He thought about it for a short while.

"I think it quite likely that they were the ones responsible for the kid's disappearance. And one prefers this idea to the notion that the lad was taken and killed by someone seeking revenge. You might also find it interesting that Beatty does a turn at the local club when they have an amateur night. He is an accomplished mimic, so that it would be easy for him to do a broad Scottish accent."

He picked up his glass and had a long draught of the beer. Fletcher sat up in his chair and began to give us an account of his activities.

"Benson certainly hates Armstrong's guts," he said. "Whatever the rights or wrongs of why the operation on him was such a disaster, he is in a poor state now and is on the bread line, living on disability benefit. He had to sell his house, since he couldn't keep up the payments on the mortgage and is now living in a tiny flat in an unpleasant part of the city. He can't talk about anything else but his hatred of Armstrong and his every fibre is intent on getting revenge on the man who, he claims, crippled him. His wife couldn't cope with his vendetta against Armstrong and has left him, which has only added fuel to his hatred for the surgeon."

"So do you think that he could have managed to do the snatching of the kid, the phone messages and the recruiting of Stalker," I asked, "if he is pretty badly disabled?"

"He can't sustain energetic activity for long periods of time," explained Fletcher. "But he can do things in short bursts, which is what would have been required in all these activities. And his hatred would give him the resolve and the strength to keep on at things even when he was finding it difficult to carry on. He has little interest in anything these days and spends a lot of his time wandering around the city. So he could have done all that was necessary in connection with the kidnapping of the lad and the later phone calls. And you will be interested to know that Benson talks with a lisp."

That last remark produced quite a reaction from the rest of us.

Fletcher returned to his beer and Marion took up the story.

"Charters, like Benson, only lives now for the getting of revenge on the person who did him out of what he regards as his rightful money, namely Mrs Armstrong," she said. "After his wife committed suicide, he had nothing whatever to look forward to except getting back at her. He still has a few friends who keep him supplied with enough cash to ensure that he can have some quality of life. So he can get around and would have been able to do all the things necessary if it was he who was the one who spirited away the kid."

"And do you think that it was he who took the kid and killed him?" I asked.

"He has the necessary drive. He really hated the Armstrong woman and used to rant about her all the time. But, since the boy was taken, he has been much quieter and more restrained. The two things could well be connected. And he speaks several languages, so it would be no problem for him to put on a marked broad Scottish accent."

We sat turning over in our minds all that had been said. After a few minutes, I spoke.

"Does anyone want to venture an opinion as to which of them did it?" I asked.

There was a silence while they decided what to do. No-one wanted to be the first to offer an opinion. It was Beaumont who broke the silence.

"It has to be Benson," he said. "The lisp gives him away. The others aren't likely to know about him and then try to implicate him by putting on a lisp when talking to Stalker."

"I am inclined to agree," said Fletcher. "I had been inclined to put my money on Beatty and Clarkson initially, but I can't see why it would take them so long to make a second ransom demand, and I can't see them being so scared that they would give up on the chance of making such a lot of money quite easily. Like Andy, I think that the lisp does it."

"And I can't see it being anyone but Benson," added Marion

I wasn't all that convinced by the arguments. I would have preferred something a bit more concrete than the lisp. But I had to agree with the others. Benson looked like the best bet.

"So I shall report all our findings to the Chief tomorrow morning," I said to them "and see what he makes of it all. If he thinks there is a good enough case to take to the

Procurator Fiscal, then that will be that."

I bought a further round and passed around my cigarettes. We discussed a few things other than the case and then Marion and I left. The other two stayed on, ordering food and further drinks. They both preferred to eat in pleasant surroundings in the company of a congenial fellow copper rather than enjoy a takeaway alone in front of the tele. But both Marion and I liked to indulge in more civilised eating.

I went up to Forsyth's office the next morning a few minutes after he had arrived. I told him everything that had emerged during the course of our discussion the previous evening and presented him with our considered conclusion. He thought about it for a few minutes and then shook his head.

"It doesn't strike me as the correct solution," he said eventually. "And I can't see the Procurator Fiscal being happy to take that case to court. There is too much that is dubious about it for him to be certain that he can get a conviction."

"I don't see what else that we can do," I pointed out. "I can't see anything further happening that will get us any nearer the truth. Now, if another demand for ransom were to come through, that would be a horse of an entirely different colour."

I had been staring at the wall as I said that and it was only when I had finished that I realised that Forsyth was sitting absolutely silent and still. I looked at him and saw that he was staring fixedly in front of him and had a constipated look on his face. I recognised that look from past experience. An idea had occurred to him and that nimble brain was giving it the once over. I sat back and waited. The great man was not to be disturbed at a moment like that.

It took a few moments for him to surface from his reverie. When he did, he looked over at me and gave me a beaming smile.

"You have this God-given ability," he suggested, "to say the key thing that unlocks in my mind the notion that contains the solution."

"You've cracked it," I said.

"I believe that I may well have done so," he admitted, trying his best to look modest and failing utterly in the attempt.

"So who did it?"

He was immediately cagey.

"Before I say anything," he told me, "there are one or two things that I have to do to confirm my theory and get the evidence that the Procurator Fiscal will need before he will be prepared to accept my solution and take the case to court."

"And what would these things be?"

"You will find that out in due course," he informed me. "And you will assist in the process. Let us go to the Armstrong residence. I trust that both will be out, one healing the sick and the other seeking to right the wrongs that the law has inflicted on innocents. You will interview Miss Clarkson and ask her as many questions as necessary to keep her occupied while I slip off and check on something in the house."

I drove him there and he was so oblivious to what was going on as he mulled over his putative solution that he did not seem to notice that I was going a little faster than I usually did and very much faster than he would normally have liked.

As Forsyth had hoped, both Armstrongs were out at work. Miss Clarkson came to the door and invited us in when I said that there were one or two things that I wished to go over with her again. I sat her down and began to ask her questions while Forsyth prowled about the room and then surreptitiously exited from it. He was gone for some time and I was beginning to run out of questions to ask and was sure that Clarkson was becoming restive at being asked the same thing in several different ways. I was therefore mightily relieved when the Chief reappeared and suggested that I had imposed on Miss Clarkson for long enough. We left and he gave me no indication as to what it was that he had been up to. He disappeared on some errand or another as soon as we reached Fettes and I saw nothing more of him that day.

It was on the following day that I was summoned to the Chief's office to find him looking cheerful and incredibly smug. I knew the signs.

"Your theory has been confirmed as you knew that it would be," I hazarded. "The Procurator Fiscal has jumped for joy at the thought of bringing such a powerful case to court and the Chief Constable has grabbed you round the neck and kissed you with tears of joy streaming down his face."

"You have got the two scenes quite wrong," he pointed out. "The Procurator Fiscal was annoyed that he would have to get his finger out and do some hard work for a change in bringing the case to court and the Chief Constable is incapable of showing any emotion at any time whatever the motivation."

"But you have brought the case to a successful conclusion?"

"I have," he said, unable to keep a hint of smugness out of his voice. "The person responsible is now languishing in durance vile."

"And are you going to reveal to me who it is?" I enquired.

"All will be revealed to you and the team this evening when I buy you drinks in the usual hostelry. Shall we say five thirty? In the meantime I have to give an interview at the BBC studios."

And with that he was off. It would have taken him just a couple of seconds to say who it was who was eating his heart out in prison at that moment. But he was not going to do anything that would detract from the impact that his revelation of the truth was to produce. We all had to be astounded by the brilliance of his reasoning and knowing the name of the guilty party might well remove some of the astonishment that his words were meant to produce.

I sighed, but it was what I had become used to and had come to expect. I went to tell the others that another case had been solved by Forsyth and that we would hear all about it over drinks in the pub.

All the facts necessary to name the person or persons who abducted James Armstrong are now in your possession. Good luck if you attempt to solve the mystery before Forsyth reveals all.

Alistair MacRae

CHAPTER 4

At 5.30 that evening, the squad was sitting at our usual table in the pub, pints of heavy in front of us. On the table at the vacant place, soon to be occupied by Forsyth, stood a large glass of his favourite malt whisky, Glenlivet. Forsyth buying us drinks is not as straightforward as it might at first seem. It is true that he will buy a round in due course, more than one if the session is prolonged. But he expects, and I always make sure, that a glass containing a Glenlivet is awaiting his arrival.

We had not been there more than a few minutes when he appeared in the doorway. He stood there and looked round the room to see where we were. Since he knows perfectly well which is the table that we always occupy, the pause in the entrance is to allow the other denizens of the bar to see which celebrity has arrived to join them. Since the inhabitants of pubs have short memories and he had not yet appeared that day, or in the recent past, on television being lauded for one of his great triumphs, his arrival caused no interest in the other drinkers whatsoever, apart from a slight disturbance at a nearby table. Unperturbed, he strolled over to our table, greeted us with a beaming smile, sat down and had a large swallow of the golden liquid from his glass. Only then did he start the evening's proceedings.

"I need hardly say," he said, "that the Chief Constable is thrilled that we have been able to find out who did the kidnapping of the child of his wife's bosom friend and wishes his heartiest congratulations to be passed on to you."

"We didn't do all that much," I pointed out.

"The efforts of the general are as nothing without the work of the foot soldiers," he intoned.

I wasn't sure that the analogy was a good one but I let it pass.

"So who was it who kidnapped the child?" asked Marion.

He smiled at her.

"All in good time," he said. "At the start of the case, we suggested that there were two possible reasons for the kidnapping, namely a desire for money or a wish for revenge. But I believe that there is a third, equally good, reason."

He paused and had another swallow of the whisky. I am sure that it was done to increase the tension. And it worked. Fletcher was forced to ask him what was that other reason.

"To safeguard the future of the young James," Forsyth explained. "Both parents were far too busy pursuing their illustrious careers to give the child the affection and attention that he so obviously needed. Miss Clarkson did her best, but she was no substitute for a loving and caring father and mother."

We were still not clear what it was that Forsyth was trying to tell us.

"So who would be so concerned about the welfare of the boy that he would take such drastic measures to change things?" enquired Marion.

"His father."

"But you just said that the father was spending too much time on his career to look to the needs of James," I pointed out.

"I am not talking about Mr Armstrong. I am talking about his real father."

"So you think that James is not Armstrong's son?" said Beaumont. "You think that his wife had an affair with someone else."

"I not only think it, I know it," said the Chief smugly and confidently.

"How can you possibly be confident that you know such a thing?" I countered. "It is not possible for you to be certain."

"It is indeed very possible. You may recall that, when we first visited the Armstrong household, we noted that both parents had cold blue eyes while the photograph of the son that she gave us showed that he had soulful brown eyes. A chance remark made by Sergeant MacRae about colour brought back to my memory these facts and reminded me that it is not possible for two blue-eyed parents to have a brown-eyed child. Such a child must have blue eyes also. Therefore, one of the Armstrongs, pretty certainly the father, was not the true parent of James."

"And Armstrong probably paid as little attention to his wife's needs as to those of his child," I suggested. "And, with a former admirer waiting in the wings, it would be almost inevitable that Mercer and Mrs Armstrong would have an affair. And, since they were careless, James was the result."

"It may well be true. It probably is," said a somewhat sceptical Beaumont. "But are you able to prove any of this?"

"There is a new technique based on the unique DNA of the individual which is starting to be used in criminal investigations. When the sergeant and I went on the last occasion to the Armstrong house, I obtained hair samples from the brushes of both parents and the child. These, when the DNA from them was analysed, showed that, while Mrs Armstrong was James' mother, Mr Armstrong could not possibly be his father. When I arrested Mercer, I obtained a sample of his hair and I can now prove beyond doubt that Mercer is the father of James."

"That is the sort of evidence that a jury can understand and will go for," I pointed out.

"You were right to find it a trifle odd that Mercer was into everything once the child was kidnapped. As you said, it was useful for him, if he was involved, to find out exactly what both the Armstrongs and the police were doing, so that he could act appropriately. Unfortunately, you did not follow that up when you found that he genuinely liked both Armstrongs and loved the son."

"And, of course," I said, "Mercer would know all about Benson and that he had a lisp, so that he could throw suspicion in that direction by imitating the defect when he spoke to Stalker."

"But Mercer was with you when the phone calls were made demanding the ransom," objected Beaumont. "How did he manage that?"

"He has a valet who has been in the family for some time, first with his father and now with him. I am sure that he is happy to do whatever his master needs, such as playing prerecorded messages into phones in various phone boxes."

"So was Mercer intending to keep the child and bring up his son himself," asked Marion, "giving him the love and affection that was so sadly lacking in the Armstrong household? But, if so, how did he expect to get away with it?"

"He had secured a top post at one of the research establishments in the USA," Forsyth explained. "He intended to smuggle James out of the country and present him to the Americans as his son from a union that was never followed by marriage. He was confident that no-one would ever question his story and he never intended to return to this country again. So he did not expect his imposture to be ever discovered or even called into question."

Since our glasses were empty, Forsyth drew some notes from his pocket and sent Fletcher to the bar to purchase large Glenlivets all round. Once we had sampled these, I asked the pertinent question.

"What exactly is Mercer being charged with? Can a father be charged with very much if he removes his son from a sterile household? And how is Armstrong coping with the knowledge that his wife and his best friend have had an adulterous relationship and the news that he is not the father of the boy whom he has been looking after, however badly, for so long?"

"Mercer is at the moment charged with the abduction of James Armstrong," the Chief announced. "But I am sure that the legal eagles will have a field day with the case and will make lots of money from arguing the rights and wrongs of what Mercer may or may not have done. It may well be that the boy would have been better off if we had never arrived at a solution of the case. But that cannot be our concern. We have a job to do and we have done it. Let others argue the legal niceties of the case. It is not our role to play God."

That was a bit of a surprise. I had been under the impression that that was what he spent a good deal of his time doing.

"And Armstrong's reaction to all that he has learned?" I asked.

"I believe that a divorce is contemplated. That may be for the best. This may make both of them reflect on their lives and on whether they have, up until this point, had their priorities correct."

A young man from the table where there had been a slight disturbance when Forsyth entered the bar came over and asked Forsyth to sign his autograph book. It was clear that the Chief was considerably chuffed that his fame was such that even the man in the street had heard of him and regarded him as a celebrity.

I am sure that it was because he was in such a good mood because of that incident that he stayed with us for another half hour, regaling us with anecdotes from his past successes and, more importantly, buying us another round of malt whiskies. And, when he finally left, he put some notes on the table so that we could continue the festivities in his absence.

Once I was sure that he had gone and was not going to return. I summoned the young man over and paid him the fiver that I had promised him.

It is, after all, one of the duties of the sergeant of a close-knit and successful team to do everything in his power to keep his boss happy and contented. It had been an unexpected bonus that this action had also secured for the team some well deserved and highly appreciated extra malt whisky.